AVOID THE MACHINES

—— A NOVEL ——

SCOTTY VASCO

CONTENTS

Introduction vii

February 12th, 2079 1
February 20th, 2079 3
February 28th, 2079 7
March 12th, 2079 11
March 17th, 2079 16
March 25th, 2079 20
April 3rd, 2079 23
April 15th, 2079 25
April 29th, 2079 32
May 25th, 2079 34
June 1st, 2079 37
June 5th, 2079 40
June 7th, 2079 43
June 10th 2079 46
June 12th, 2079 49
June 16th, 2079 51
June 20th, 2079 57
June 28th, 2079 60
July 3rd, 2079 62

July 7th, 2079.. 64
July 10th 2079.. 67
July 13th, 2079... 73
July 14th, 2079 Revolution Time 77
Three Days Later: July 17th, 2079 117
4 Days Later: July 21st, 2079 130
One Month Later: August 21st, 2079.............................. 132

INTRODUCTION

THE YEAR IS 2084, AND copies of a pamphlet by a member of an organization who call themselves the Nouvo Saracens have become collector's items around the world. The pamphlet was written five years earlier by a revolutionary organizer named Mike Mackandal. The manuscript was written as a daily journal, documenting the day to day planning and strategizing of Mackandal. But after the Melanin Rebellion in 2079, many supporters and admirers of Mackandal converted the journal into booklet form to spread as a source of inspiration to oppressed people globally.

FEBRUARY 12ᵗʰ, 2079

M Y NAME IS MICHAEL MAKANDAL. I'm a 32-year-old former accounts manager at an advertising agency here in New York City. I'm writing this journal to document my mission in the event that I was to disappear.

In five months from now, we are going to do something that has never been done on this soil. We are going to start a full out Black armed revolution.

People have talked about carrying out a Black revolution for decades on this soil. But they have never followed through. Some of this has to do with fear. In some cases, it was lack of proper planning. In some cases, it was a betrayal. And in most cases, it was because of immediate defeat by the oppressor class.

But a successful revolution against an oppressor class is possible, and it has worked. Places like Haiti, Algeria, Vietnam, and others were successful in fighting off and defeating their oppressors who had superior military firepower.

One of the first rules of warfare is deciding how far you are going to go with the war before you begin. I'm willing to fight to the death, and I want others around me who has the same mindset.

Black people engage in episodes of temporary property damage every now and then when they get fed up with non-justice. But these little small-scale riots mean nothing if you still allow the entire system of white supremacy to remain intact. We have to completely destroy that system or die trying.

We are going to learn from the failures and successes of revolutions in the past to assist us with our mission. And we plan to launch our attack on a specific date: July 14th, 2079.

Why July 14th? This date has a symbolic significance. July 14th was the original date set for the Denmark Vesey slave rebellion that was going to take place in Charleston South Carolina in 1822. That uprising was thwarted by traitors within the Black society at that time. But Denmark Vesey- who was actually a free Black man during the time of the planned rebellion, planned with his followers to kill every white slaveholder in Charleston. Even as a so-called "free Black man," Vesey understood that living in a complete system of white supremacy, under the total domination of the white oppressor class, was still slavery. And there is only one way to get out from under that system.

We are going to complete Denmark Vesey's mission.

. . . .

FEBRUARY 20th, 2079

IT'S 9:48 PM AND I just made it back to my condominium in midtown before the unofficial 10pm curfew. There is a general understanding that the police in New Albion will harass or arrest any Black person who is out on the streets after 10pm. I was over at one of the townships going over some strategies with some of my trusted revolutionary comrades.

For anyone unfamiliar with the townships, these are areas that were created for Black society after World War 3. After WW3 in the year 2032, the United States merged with Canada and Mexico. This newly designated land mass was named New Albion.

That name Albion must have some type of sentimental significance to the white supremacists because Albion was the original name of England. And many believe that this is the origin of the term albino, which describes de-pigmented people.

And this is what the system of white supremacy is all about: de-pigmented people with a form of albinism, creating a system of domination, control, and mistreatment of the melanated people on the planet. This is done ultimately to ensure the genetic bloodline of the albino population.

In the nation of New Albion, people classified as white make up less than 15% of the population. Over the past 40 years, there was a rapid natural decrease of the white population. The white supremacists tried several strategies and policies to increase the white race population. They tried different forms of cloning. But that backfired because many of the people they cloned had severe psychological issues, and many of them engaged in spontaneous and random mass shootings. And most of the victims were white. So that defeated the purpose.

There were also policies put in place to re-classify other previously non-white racial group categories. So, all the Asians and Hispanics in New Albion were re-classified as white. But this began to further "degrade" (in their ideology) the white bloodline. This is because most people who were classified as Hispanic had African bloodlines. And these throwback genes would randomly show up when Hispanic whites intermixed with Anglo whites. And the Asian intermixing was having an adverse effect on the white bloodlines as well. Plus, many Asians saw the white population declining as an opportunity for them to have more solidarity with other Asian groups and acquire more resources.

The Black population was forced into small, concentrated areas called townships. The name and concept of townships were popularized in South Africa in the middle 20th century. In order for the white minority to survive among a Black majority in South Africa, they had to create an apartheid system, which is nothing but another word for white supremacy.

In the white minority controlled South Africa, the Black population was denied and deprived of equal resources and they were funneled into impoverished concentration camp styled ghettos called townships. Even though there were uprisings and rebellions in those South African townships for years, the white minority maintained order and control over the large Black population there for decades.

In the year 2028, the white population in South Africa dwindled down to 6%. The political figures along with the media staged a few anti-white attacks from alleged Black radicals, and they created a propaganda campaign behind the backlash.

So, between April 13th and April 23rd of that year, the white supremacists went on a mass extermination purge and systematically murdered the majority of the Black population living in the townships in South Africa. At first, they poisoned the water supply. Then they proceeded to use airborne bioweapons designed to target individuals with certain levels of melanin. These chemicals did the most damage because that immediately wiped out 70% of the Black population in the townships almost overnight.

The Black South Africans who did not die from the bioweapons and the ones who were labeled as radicals who chose to fight back at the last minute were simply gunned down on sight. Consequently, this did little actually to increase the Anglo white population there. Their numbers only increased by 4% in the immediate years following the native African purge.

To increase their numbers, the white supremacists in

South Africa started to create immigration incentives for Asians to come into the country. Once the Asians arrived, they were re-classified as white. And this is where the white supremacists who control New Albion got their policy from.

The term ghetto had too much of an overtly negative connotation. So many of the ghettos in New Albion were simply renamed "townships", as a way to give the illusion of a non-military occupied, democratic state for African people. More township ghettos were being constructed in order to house the Black masses.

The townships in New Albion also operate as holding centers for Blacks to ultimately be sent to the prison system. The white supremacists in power deliberately deprive the overcrowded townships of resources. And they fully understand the result of this will be the formation of a criminal class.

This deliberate and systematic orchestration of a Black criminal class by the white supremacists has resulted in the greater incarceration of over 9 million Black people in the prison system in New Albion.

I, along with my revolutionary comrades, plan to help liberate all 9 million of them.

. . . .

FEBRUARY 28th, 2079

I T'S 8:15 PM. MY MOOD is somewhat numb at the moment. I usually get this feeling when I visit the gravesite of my wife and son. I made my monthly trip to the cemetery today at 3pm. I wanted to get in and get out in time before I got caught up in traffic.

I have gone through so many extreme emotions in the past 2 years since their death. Sadness. Anger. A feeling of helplessness. And now I just feel numb. I have literally purged out all my emotions. And that's a good thing. You can see things with more clarity when your emotions are not distracting you.

After I left the cemetery, I met up with another one of my revolutionary comrades, Zedelph at a cafe not too far from the Sylvester Township in Long Island. Zedelph is a retired military vet, who has excellent training in airborne and hand to hand combat. Zedelph and I met at a gun range many years back, and he is one of the few people that I have a major level of trust for.

I make it a point to always meet with comrades in a public location. The New Albion government has technology where they can remotely turn on almost any electrical device in your home and record the conversation. They also have covert surveillance towers in almost every major city. These towers that look like normal electrical poles are programmed to pick up on certain word phrases from people having conversations outside. So if a person spoke a certain phrase such as "kill the president" or "we need to rise up" for example, this would put authorities on alert. So, meeting in public places where multiple conversations are taking place, makes it harder for surveillance towers to hone in on specific conversations.

Today at our meeting, Zedelph and I discussed recruiting people from the townships around New Albion who could join us on our mission. We were going over different vetting processes we could use for new potential recruits.

Zedelph was very instrumental in my decision to carry out this July 14th revolution. 5 months ago, Zedelph got access to a military document provided to him by one of his trusted colleagues in the army. This document laid out in detail how the government had a plan to systematically exterminate about 75% of the Black population in New Albion.

After Zedelph shared the document with me, I knew that there had to be some sort of action taken. In too many cases throughout history, different marginalized ethnic groups just sat around and basically waited on their genocide. In Nazi Germany back in the 20th century, the Jewish population marched obediently into those concentration camps and gas chambers. The Jewish people waited until the last train to the concentration camp was set to arrive before they took any significant action to fight back. By then it was too late.

And the situation that happened to the Black people in South Africa still baffles me to this day. The Black population there was the majority. And for decades they allowed the white supremacist to funnel them into poor townships, where they were deprived of resources, while the minority white population lived in luxury for the most part. The Black South Africans just allowed this to happen until the white supremacists decided to liquidate the townships and wipe out most of the Black population.

Why didn't the Black South Africans simply kill the white supremacist minority population? They should have slaughtered them a long time ago. What did the Black population there have to lose? They were already dirt poor, with no land, and no resources. The white supremacists took all the best farming lands there for themselves and pushed the African natives into barren ghettos. The Black South Africans should have killed every single white supremacist there when they had a chance. They had literally nothing to lose and everything to gain. Yet they remained complicit in their subjugation and were ultimately exterminated in large numbers.

This will not happen to us here in New Albion.

Some of the recruitment strategies Zedelph and I discussed during our meeting at the cafe, required potential comrades to commit certain acts of vandalism. "Potential recruits would have to test their loyalty to the movement and the mission by committing small crimes that targeted law enforcement," I suggested while trying to keep my voice down in this crowded cafe that was filled with mostly white people. "New recruits would have to flatten the tires of police vehicles. And some would have to spray paint profanities outside on the walls of police stations."

"I think we should test the loyalty of potential fighters by having them actually kill a cop," Zedelph responded. "We need to have serious charges to hang over the heads of potential recruits if they ever think about betraying the mission."

"That's an overreach," I said. "If potential recruits start killing cops as an initiation process, that will put law enforcement all over the country on high alert." Zedelph was listening and taking mental notes.

"We don't need to bring any unnecessary heat on us or the mission before we spring into action," I said, reminding him to think about every logical angle.

"We also need to screen potential recruits by verifying who their immediate family members are," Zedelph suggested. "That way, if they collaborate with the enemy, they will know that we can get to them or their family."

"I agree. And again, I think having them do petty crimes against police property will be enough to test their commitment and use as a form of insurance against them if they break rank," I said.

Zedelph and I talked at the cafe for an additional 30 minutes until I had to leave and head home. I needed to get as much rest as possible. I have to get up bright and early to check the prices for tractors and bulldozers.

MARCH 12th, 2079

T'S 9:17 AM. I'M HAVING breakfast and watching the 24-hour news channel right now. I'm still a little groggy from getting in from a late drive last night. I drove 2 hrs. both ways yesterday from New York to Allentown, PA.

I drove down there to meet with one of our comrades, David. David is a 37-year-old electrician originally from Philadelphia who comes from a mixed-race background. Even though David is classified as Black, he is light enough to pass for white, depending on the hairstyle he chooses to wear.

Allentown has one of the largest gun shows in the country this time of year. And like most gun shows held around the country, these are places where many hardcore white extremists link up to purchase weapons without having to do background checks. The merchants at these gun shows are generally well versed in certain legal loopholes that can be implemented to purchase unregistered weapons as well.

New Albion has a federal gun law that contains a loophole that says citizens are allowed 30 days to register firearms that are purchased from private sellers in certain cities in 3 different states. Allentown is one of those cities.

The federal gun laws have been modified to disarm the Black masses. And many of the loopholes were put in place so that white supremacists could get easy access to weapons to arm themselves. That's where David comes in.

Because David has the ability to "pass," we are going to have him go into the Allentown gun show and purchase a cache of weapons. This strategy isn't new. This technique was used back in the year 1906 during the Atlanta Race Riots. The white supremacists there came up with a trumped-up justification to attack the innocent Black citizens of Atlanta. The goal was to ultimately drive the Black people out of the Atlanta area so it would be an all-white enclave. At the time, there was a gun ban for the Black citizens of Atlanta. So that left many Black people there in a vulnerable position, and a lot of innocent Black men, women, and children were killed.

So, the Black people there who were a part of the underground economy took it upon themselves to come up with solutions to fight back. They gave money to the Black mulattos who could pass for white and had them go into the gun stores to get weapons. And they used those weapons to fight off white supremacist citizens and well as the police in Atlanta in order to protect Black society there at the time. So, we make it a point to get several "passable" Black people involved in missions such as this.

I went to Allentown to drop the money off to David. David purchased the guns from the gun show. He then dropped the weapons off to another comrade who drove into Allentown from Ohio. The guns are taken to Cleveland and stored there. We usually rotate people like this because it is more difficult for law enforcement to track the activities of multiple people who are on the same page.

We chose Ohio as one of the central locations for our weapons storage because it is in the center of New Albion. So, if we were to need reinforcements during our mission, we could quickly reach Ohio from the North, South, East and West regions of the country. The high-speed sonic train system takes less than 3 hours to reach Ohio from any direction in New Albion. So, we have several "safe houses" there.

As I'm watching the news channel, a story flashes across the screen about a 16-year-old Black girl who was killed by two white law enforcement officials. The report claimed the child was walking home from school, and she was mistaken for a robbery suspect from days earlier, and the race soldiers, acting as police, simply executed her. On average, about one Black youth is killed each week by race soldiers in New Albion. And if the killer is classified as white, that person will not be charged with a crime.

The New Albion government has openly embraced the old United States Supreme Court ruling on the Dred Scott decision. In 1857 the US Supreme Court ruled that Black people in America were inferior to whites and that a Black man had no rights that a white man was bound to respect. This court decision was thoroughly enforced, and it was never overturned. Many people would argue that the Dred Scott decision was overturned by the 14th Amendment of the US Constitution. This amendment was also transferred over to the New Albion government when this country was established.

The 14th Amendment states that it gives equal

protection under the law to Black citizens. But that's simply not true. Black citizens were treated unfairly compared to white citizens in every area of the society during and after the constitutional amendments.

And Black citizens are still legally executed by race soldiers for any trivial reason. White citizens are not randomly murdered by law enforcement, even when they commit heinous crimes. So there has never been equal treatment or protection under the law. The 14th Amendment was simply never fully enforced.

But the Supreme Court Dred Scott decision is fully enforced.

And Black people as a whole don't seem to understand that we are in a complete system of white supremacy where it is a cultural duty for the white supremacist to harm, dominate, and mistreat people who are classified as non-white in general, and Black people in particular. And nothing they do to Black people, no matter how insidious and unjust, is considered a crime.

As I continued to watch the news coverage of the case of the 16-year-old child being killed, they announced that Black organizations would have a protest over the shooting this week. I had to shake my head to this. Black people have to realize; we are long past the era of protesting white supremacy. Protesting simply doesn't work anymore. Who are they protesting to? They are not protesting to get the attention of other Black people. Because they are just victims of white supremacy too. So Black people protest to get the attention of white people. And even though all white people are not racist, unfortunately, the whites who believe in maintaining white supremacy are the most powerful people on the planet. And enough people classified as white are fully on board with the systematic subjugation and mistreatment of Black people.

So, these protests are falling on deaf ears. There is a hateful indifference from the dominant white society of New Albion to the mistreatment of Black citizens. So, protests are a complete waste of time, and it is looked upon as a nuisance to white society. This is why Black people have to change their strategies. These race soldiers have to be killed.

That's the only way to get people to stop oppressing you. You have to be willing to administer repercussions, even if it puts your life on the line, to anyone who will not stop oppressing and mistreating you. And violence is the only weapon that can be used against the white supremacists.

MARCH 17th, 2079

TODAY I AM ON MY way to a church to pick up money from Reverend Randal Prescott. The reverend is one of several pastors who is working covertly with our revolution movement. Reverend Prescott was affiliated with several so-called "militant" organizations before he became a pastor. About 20 years ago, he was covertly involved with a series of police station bombings on the West Coast.

When it looked like the heat was about to turn up on him, he became a Christian minister. He became one of the most well respected Black ministers in all of New Albion. Even though Reverend Prescott is popular among Black and white audiences, he still secretly holds on to his revolutionary mindset.

Our organization is getting financial resources by working with revolutionary Christian pastors who share our vision. Reverend Prescott is giving me $15,000 cash so I can purchase more weapons for our comrades in the townships. I have been receiving similar cash allocations from other church leaders around the country, who are covertly assisting with our mission. The good thing about

16

collaborating with these churches is that the cash we receive is untraceable

The Denmark Vesey rebellion that was planned in the early 1800's utilized the same strategy. Vesey and his followers hid their agenda under the guise of attending regular church services. When they went to these church services, they planned their attack strategies, and they accumulated resources needed to carry out their planned rebellion. The thing that thwarted the Denmark Vesey rebellion was the fact that Vesey and his followers underestimated the negro collaborators in the system of white supremacy. It was the coons and sell-outs who sabotaged that rebellion. We are not going to have that problem when we carry out our mission.

Another reason why I have a certain level of trust for Reverend Prescott is that the reverend knows I have some dirt on him. Law enforcement officials are not fully aware of Reverend Prescott's involvement with the police station bombings decades ago. But we have info and eyewitnesses who can directly implicate Reverend Prescott. So, the reverend knows if he were to snitch or try to sabotage our mission, we have information that would bury him.

But I know we would never get to that level because the reverend has been a stand-up guy for a long time. He was even the pastor who presided over the funeral service for my wife and son.

2 years ago, while I was at work, my wife was driving home with my 7-year-old son in the back seat. A race soldier employed as a police officer pulled my wife over for what he claimed was an "improper turn." He went up to the car and asked my wife for her registration. When she reached for the glove compartment to get the documents, the race

soldier pulled out his weapon and began firing in the car, killing my wife and my son.

This race soldier was never charged because he claimed he feared for his life when my wife reached for the registration that he asked for. Not only was the officer not charged with a crime, but he also raised over 4 million dollars in donations from white supremacists all over New Albion. This type of outpouring of support is one of the motivating factors behind race soldiers executing unarmed Black citizens: They will be rewarded financially for it and not be punished.

But all of that is going to change.

Until my wife and child were killed, I, like every other Black person in New Albion, sat back and just waited on these white supremacists to fade away. I sat back with a neglectful indifference about the things happening to other Black people in New Albion. I remained stagnant hoping that other people would handle the issue of race soldiers systematically harming Black citizens.

But we have allowed this racial mistreatment to go on long enough, and we don't make a fuss about it until it directly affects us. Black people have fooled themselves into believing that this system of white supremacy is going to one day treat us collectively equal. The white supremacists are good at taking one Black person and showering that person with praises, accolades and sometimes personal resources. And other Black people are taught to live vicariously through that one individual Black person while the Black masses suffer from systematic deprivation.

The reality is, too many Black people have grown comfortable under the subjugation of the white supremacists. And now our complacency is about to lead to our extermination. This is why it is imperative for us to take specific action on a specific date. No more of that "one day it will get better" talk that Black people have been praying about for the last few centuries.

We are going to make things right by making things even.

MARCH 25th, 2079

TODAY WE HAD A MEETING in one of the townships. Zedelph and I met with some of the local drug dealers. Some of our other comrades in other cities have been conducting similar meetings throughout townships all over New Albion. Our mission is to get some of these street guys on board with our agenda.

Zedelph used to work with gang intervention organizations some years back, so a lot of the people in the underworld have a general level of trust for him. And Zedelph knows how to avoid the drug dealers who are potential snitches. He is able to do this because there are many drug dealers who make a conscious decision to work with law enforcement to move narcotics throughout the townships. Zedelph had connections that gave him access to the police department's database of criminal suspects. Through the database, we could find out which drug dealers were informants and which ones cut deals with law enforcement. We are going to work with the dealers who are least likely to collaborate with the white supremacists.

It may seem counter-productive, on a surface level, for

us to be working with drug dealers who many people say "sells poison to other Black people." But when it comes to a serious revolution, all people can be utilized. Every Black person in New Albion and the world for that matter are in a global, societal prison. Every one of us is subjugated and dominated by the white supremacists. And within any prison system, no prisoner is above the other. We are told that there are Black people who are not like the others, and this keeps us divided within the societal prison.

The system of white supremacy does not need 4 walls and bars in order to create a prison system. They have mastered the art of making entire societies prisons. This is evident in places like Ukraine in the early 1930's. Joseph Stalin wanted to rid the society of the "ethnic Ukrainians," so he orchestrated a man-made famine historically referred to as The Holodomor.

During the Holodomor, officials disarmed the Ukrainian people and closed the borders so that people could not come in or get out. Then officials began to deprive the people of resources. They would not allow food into the closed-off societies, and they would not allow people to grow their own food. Consequently, between 7 and 10 million people ultimately died of starvation.

Currently we are in a similar societal prison. And we have remained in this globally radicalized prison for so long, the white supremacists are now planning to "liquidate" the inhabitants of the prison. This is why every non-white victim of systematic white supremacy is needed to destroy this system.

And when it comes to total and complete liberation, we have to be guided by practicality and not have our vision clouded by morality. Most of society look at the drug dealers from a moral standpoint. But we revolutionaries look at them from a practical standpoint. The pros of working with certain drug dealers are:

1. They generally have access to untraceable cash
2. They generally have access to untraceable weapons
3. They understand the importance of having a code. Because there are certain street codes one must abide by
4. They are already considered "outsiders" by mainstream society. So, they will have fewer reservations about attacking the system
5. They have access to drug users, who are deemed as outsiders, who can be utilized to carry out strategic missions.

The drug of choice that is extremely popular in the streets right now is a narcotic called Foam. This drug is purchased in a form that resembles a small stick of gum. It has a soft, chalky texture. The user ads a teaspoon of hydrogen peroxide to the substance, then it turns into a small foam configuration. After around 20 seconds the foam hardens. Once the foam hardens, users can chip off small chunks and put each chunk in glass pipes to smoke. And one $40 foam ball can be broken down and used all day. And users say the high is more intense than cocaine and crystal meth combined.

Foam is highly addictive and "foam heads" are willing to do anything to get their fix of the drug. We are going to use this reality to our advantage.

APRIL 3rd, 2079

JUST GOT BACK FROM A meeting with one of our hackers who is down with the cause. Kelton Rose has been hacking into computers, banking and military systems for years. Kelton did three years in the penitentiary for hacking into the computer systems of several escrow companies. He laundered seventeen million dollars in the course of 2 months. He is the only Black person in the history of New Albion who was convicted of laundering that much money.

Once Kelton was release from prison, he has been under constant surveillance by the FBI, and his online activities are heavily monitored. This is why he primarily navigates online using the Dark Web. The Dark Web allows users to surf online without being easily detected. And because of this, the Dark Web is used to conduct many types of illegal and illicit activities.

Users can purchase drugs, guns, explosives, credit card, passports, and every other thing you can imagine, online using the Dark Web. Kelton has used the Dark Webs to set up untraceable email addresses for us. This way we can communicate and correspond with each other nationwide without the threat of prying eyes from the FEDS.

Kelton has also set up physical addresses which can receive untraceable semi-automatic guns and hand grenades. He is also arranging for us to get dozens of small, untraceable bulldozers. We are also going to need large trucking containers to transport these bulldozers. We are going to utilize these vehicles to break as many Black inmates out of prison as possible.

For centuries, Black people have just sat around and allowed this racialized mass incarceration of Black citizens happen. Now, this mass incarceration is turning into a mass extermination. And at this point, we have absolutely nothing to lose. So, we are going to do what should have been done a long time ago. We are going to send comrades to every prison in New Albion and literally tear down the walls on July 14th.

Some of the comrades felt that Kelton was a risky ally at first, because of law enforcement shadowing his activities. Some people thought that this could be an incentive for him to flip and snitch on the movement. But Kelton did those three years in prison without ratting anyone out, even though prosecutors offered him multiple deals and early freedom. He knows how to keep his mouth shut. Plus, he despises race soldiers within law enforcement because he witnessed his younger brother get executed by one of them when he was a teen.

So, Kelton is going to be a great asset to our movement as far as getting the tools needed for this revolution.

APRIL 15th, 2079

ZEDELPH AND I ARE FLYING back to New Albion from Eredo Africa. Eredo was the name of Nigeria before it was colonized by the British in the 1800's. After the Nigerian revolution in 2059, when the Nigerians kicked out all the white supremacists and took back control of their land and oil reserves, they renamed the area Eredo. We had a very important meeting while we were in that country.

We brought one of our comrades who is an economist with us named Christopher Roy. Christopher was one of the few Black people who worked with me at the advertising agency. He worked in the accounts payable department, which was a position he was over-qualified for, based on the number of degrees he had. Last year, the white supremacists at the job concocted a bogus reason to fire him. They blamed some non-existent "accounting discrepancy" on him, and simply terminated him. What I later found out is that one of the white supervisors at the agency wanted to open up a position for one of his relatives who was in need of a job at the time. I quit the agency shortly after that because I knew my days would be numbered there as well.

I took my savings and opened up a number of coin-operated laundromats around New York City. This has been my primary income since. And the good thing about having the laundromats is that it allows me to stay under the radar while I bring in an income.

Christopher has helped me with my accounting and books, and we have established a certain level of trust. This is why we brought him to Eredo Africa with us. While in Eredo, we had an off the record meeting with the President of that country, Daniel Odita. Zedelph has a lot of political ties to Eredo through his family, who are of Nigerian descent. This is how we were able to get our foot in the door with President Odita.

With every revolution, it is always important to have international allies. That is one thing that Black people in New Albion never established. There have been several rebellions and uprisings on this soil, but there cannot be a true revolution until the rebels can sustain themselves economically.

President Odita discussed with us the importance of establishing international trade with Eredo. When Eredo forcefully gained its real independence from Britain, Western powers constantly tried to sabotage its economic growth. When Eredo was called Nigeria, they were independent on paper, but they were still economically colonized by Western interests. The terms "Western interests", and "Western powers", are just euphemisms for white supremacists, to be clear.

When the people of Eredo expelled all the white supremacists and took back control of their land, oil, gold, and other resources, Britain, New Albion and other Western powers imposed trade sanctions on Eredo. But Eredo has been able to maintain significant trade deals with Arab and Asian countries, so their economy is fairly stable at this point. And Eredo is the only African country that has opened its doors to Black people from the diaspora to return and gain citizenship. And their military is sufficient enough to protect the integrity and safety of their citizens.

But President Odita understands that his country needs a more advanced military presence. Eredo needs access to the new atomic and laser weapon military intelligence that Western countries have. And he understands that he needs more African minds that can help come up with new forms of military resources and weaponry, independent of the Western nations. And we have been assisting President Odita with this mission.

We have been sending some of our potential rebels down to Cuba to learn science and medicine. Back in the early 2000's, Cuba announced that they would allow Black people from North America to go to Cuba and go to school to learn medicine free of charge. Some years after this, Cuba expanded the free scholarship program to include business and management. And Cuba still has this policy today for any Black person in New Albion to go to school there and study.

So, we have a team of Black comrades who were educated in Cuba as well as parts of New Albion, who have the revolutionary mindset, and are ready to work with us and the Eredo government. And our economist Christopher Roy is presenting some strategies on ways we can funnel money in from New Albion to Eredo without violating the trade sanctions. Some of the strategies Christopher discussed with President Odita was setting up NGOs in Eredo and quietly transferring money through these organizations in various ways.

We plan on sending the government of Eredo at least 8 million dollars within the next two months. The Eredo government already allows Black people from the diaspora to get free parcels of land if they chose to live there. So, the money we are sending will assist with building a modest number of homes in the areas designated for expatriates. Also, the money we send to Eredo will show them that we are very serious about our mission, and this is a way to earn the trust of the Eredo government.

The government of New Albion has sent in several secret agents to Eredo to make assassination attempts on the life of President Odita. Western powers have always targeted African leaders who did not want to act as puppets for the white supremacists.

So, we have to make sure that we have proven ourselves to be trustworthy to the government there. The fact that Zedelph has family members who still live in Eredo, and they have a relationship with President Odita, it's a huge plus for us. The Eredo government has opened its doors to Black expatriates from around the globe, and they are still working on better ways to vet the people who are coming there to live. To help avoid Black people from New Albion who are agents of the white supremacists from coming in to sabotage the infrastructure of Eredo, President Odita is looking into new practical as well as technological strategies. One strategy is to require that some expats prove their lineage can trace back to indigenous land there.

Another strategy is to require expats to invest a certain

sum of capital into the infrastructure of Eredo. For people who cannot trace their ancestry to the land, and if they don't have the money to invest into the economy, they are required to get an electronic tattoo. This is a tattoo that's usually placed on the bottom leg or the shoulder of a person. An electronic tattoo looks like a normal tattoo, but this type of tattoo has small electronic fiber optics embedded in the ink. And the tattoo can be tracked and monitored anywhere in the world. If the Eredo government finds out that an expatriate is secretly collaborating with enemy entities, the government can track the traitor, and send an electric volt to the tattoo killing the person instantly. The electronic tattoo is taken off an expatriate after 10 years. This process will ensure that a person is not coming into the country of Eredo as an agent or provocateur.

We discussed several other strategies and policies we should use with Eredo- the only current African nation that is not afraid to stand up against their oppressive colonizers. During our meeting with President Odita, he made a very interesting suggestion: "What is your name," President Odita asked as he looked over at me while we were sitting in his personal library room. "Michael Makandal," I replied confusingly because I knew he was familiar with all of our names at this point. "No, no, no. I know *your* name", President Odita said as he chuckled. "I'm asking about the name of your organization. What do you call yourselves?

Zedelph, Christopher and I looked at each other with stumped expressions. "We really don't have a name," Zedelph said, chiming in. "We have been so caught up in doing community work, we haven't given it much thought." President Odita sat back in his chair and thought for a few seconds. "You brothers need a name. Something known among your immediate circle. The work you are doing is so powerful; you should have some type of title that will solidify your movement."

We listened to Odita with intense curiosity. Christopher looked over at the President and said: "I think one of the reasons why we haven't named ourselves, is because we understand the necessity of being extremely discreet." Odita nodded his head in agreement. "You can be discreet and carry out your mission and still have an unofficial title among yourselves. This will have a powerful impact among the people within your movement," President Odita replied.

Odita looked over at me and said: "you should call yourselves the Nouvo Saracens." Zedelph, Christopher and I looked at each other trying to understand what that name meant. Odita then elaborated on the name. "The Saracens were Africans who were part of the Moorish conquest that took place in Medieval Europe. I see that same spirit of conquest with your movement," Odita said.

"What's the Nouvo reference?", I asked. "Well, the independence of my country was inspired by the Haitian Revolution that took place in the 1800's," Odita said. He continued, "the Haitian Creole word for "new" is "nouvo". So, in the spirit of the Moorish conquest and the Haitian Revolution, you should call yourselves the Nouvo Saracens."

After Odita broke that information down to us, we absolutely loved the idea of the name. We discussed many other intricate details of our plans with President Odita over the next few hours. We departed from the meeting and headed directly to the airport. On our flight home, we discussed our new name and all the details of the meeting we had with President Odita. This trip has motivated us more than ever.

The Nouvo Saracens are ready for revolution.

APRIL 29th, 2079

TODAY THERE WERE A SERIES of meetings in townships all over New Albion about training pit bulls. In almost every township you go to, there are several people there who own pit bull dogs. Some of our Nouvo Saracen members are amateur dog breeders/trainers as well. We are going to use these dogs to our advantage when the time comes.

The name of the game is to weaponizing everything. Everything we touch is going to be used for our empowerment. That includes our pets.

This afternoon, I am also going talk with our main computer hacker, Kelton Rose about how we can use over-the-counter drones during the revolution. We had a short discussion about using the drones on our weekly 2-way radio briefing a few days ago. One of the other Nouvo Saracen members who was in on that discussion is another ex-military man, and he mentioned that the government has ways to scramble the signals of drones and render them disabled. So, if anyone can find a way to override any type of military interference with our drones, Kelton Rose is the guy.

Kelton and a team of his hand-picked hackers are also working on getting the names and addresses of every single race soldier in New Albion who has been exonerated for killing innocent or unarmed Black people. They have hacked into the police database in cities all over the country and obtained employment, and personal info of officers involved in these executions and cover-ups. They have also obtained information of all the police union leaders around New Albion who protect the race soldiers who get away with executing unarmed Black people. When the revolution starts, we are going to target all of these people first. We are then going to target all the white supremacist civilians who have been exonerated for killing innocent, unarmed Black people.

Kelton and his team also hacked into court system records and obtained the names and addresses of judges, prosecutors, and jurors who have assisted race soldiers in getting away with executing innocent Black people. We are going after them as well. All of these communities that have a code of protecting and harboring people involved with the oppression and death of Black people in New Albion are in our crosshairs.

For years, Black people have cowardly allowed these white supremacists and race soldiers target and harm Black men, women, and children with impunity. And Black people have marched, begged, and cried to the white supremacists for centuries in an effort to convince them to stop. And this method has not worked. And now it has led to a planned genocide.

Now, the Nouvo Saracens are not asking or begging the white supremacists to stop harming us. We are going to make them stop.

MAY 25th, 2079

N AN EFFORT TO RAISE more money, we have recruited some Black people to act as double agents against the white supremacists. Some months back, we started scouting for Black people who were somewhat media savvy. After a thorough screening and vetting process, Zedelph and I decided to groom a gentleman named Gerald Harris. He was the first of 5 other people we are recruiting for this particular mission.

Gerald is a bright 24-year-old college graduate who would correspond with us in some of our encrypted chat room discussions on the deep web. He was invited to the discussions by another one of our trusted associates. Gerald had a knack for locating hard to find documents and information on police officers. He would provide valuable information to us whenever we would brainstorm for ideas. And he was willing to personally kill a white judge who sentenced his cousin to life in prison for a bogus drug conviction if we provided the weapon for him.

One of the Nouvo Saracen members gave him an untraceable pistol with a silencer on it, and Gerald discreetly killed the judge and the judge's wife. And he somehow disposed of the bodies, to where they have never been found. There were reports on the news for weeks of the missing judge, and how they were stumped over his disappearance. We did not want Gerald to disclose to the locations of the bodies to any Nouvo Saracen members, because we wanted to maintain plausible deniability in case anything went down before the revolution.

In addition to his dedication to the movement, once Zedelph and I met Gerald in person, we saw that he had a very charismatic demeanor. We decided he was charismatic enough to be groomed to go conservative media outlets and act as a double agent.

The dominant society has always propped up Black people who act as mascots for white supremacy. Many white supremacists will co-opt Black people to act as shields for them. They will offer some type of incentive, whether it's money, a job title or position, or simply white acceptance, to Black people who will regurgitate their racist talking points for them. And the white supremacists are always scouting for Black people who engage in derogatory rhetoric about other Black people.

We decided we are going to use this to our advantage.

We had Gerald gain online notoriety by making a series of videos criticizing Black people in the townships for "not taking personal responsibility for their own conditions." After many of his videos went viral, many national news and media outlets began to have him on their television programs to recite the same anti-Black rhetoric. He quickly became a hit among white supremacists viewers. We had Kelton Rose set up a website for Gerald that had an option to receive monetary contributions, and donations started pouring in. We received hundreds of thousands of dollars every time Gerald would get on television and deny the existence of systematic white supremacy and change the subject to "Black on Black crime." Many white supremacists try to trick themselves into believing they are not racists if they get a Black person to spew the racist venom for them.

The money we received from Gerald's website was used to purchase more weapons and ammunition, and we started funneling some of the money to the government of Eredo Africa. Also, some of that money, along with our other financial sources, was used to purchase more solar powered RV vehicles. Because when the revolution starts, we have to be mobile and constantly on the move.

There were a few other Black people we groomed like Gerald, to act as double agent mascots for white supremacy. And not only did their media appearances bring in additional funds, they were also able to gain intel on the inner workings of these white supremacist media outlets. They were able to get names and photos of producers who worked behind the scenes at these networks, and they were also able to map out the interior of these studios. They gave us insight on the check-in and security measures needed to get into these networks. This was important because when the revolution starts, we are targeting the white supremacist media too. Many of the people in charge of that sector are going to die.

JUNE 1st, 2079

AFTER A SERIES OF RIGID grooming, scouting, and vetting, the Nouvo Saracens are up to 500 members strong. There were some potential recruits who were suspected of being potential snitches or informants.

They were immediately killed.

We have a zero-tolerance policy for potential turncoats. And we have sent a message loud and clear to other members, that if you collaborate with our oppressors against us, you will be brutally terminated. This is from the Harriet Tubman school of thought. During antebellum slavery, Harriet Tubman would lead groups of runaway slaves to freedom by traveling through different underground networks to free states. And she took a gun with her that she used to threaten to kill slaves with if they turned around and went back to the slave plantations. She did this because she knew if they went back to the plantations, they would tell on all the other Black people who were trying to escape. So, once we get a recruit who has a general idea of what the mission goal is, and they give us any reason to suspect that they might betray our plans, we terminate that recruit.

This week, we have members around the country scouting the areas in their cities for power grids and water supplies. We are going to target these public utility sources as well. We have recruited several people from the New Albion armed forces, including several brothers from the Air Force. We are also setting up training for civilian rebel members to get plane and helicopter flying lessons. All of this is going to come in handy on the day of revolution.

We also have members near the coast of Florida who are securing large boats for us to use. Some of the drug dealers from the townships are using their South American connections to get additional cargo shipping vessels. These boats are equipped with magnetic radar scrambling devices, so that they can sail the oceans without being easily detected. These boats are large enough to bring over thousands of people at a time, and they are equipped to sail under the radar for long periods of time. The day of the revolution we are going to have boatloads of people from Haiti and Cuba brought over here to New Albion to assist us with our mission.

We have also made sure that Nouvo Saracen members are stocked up on two way and HAM radios. We have given everyone a designated frequency to transmit from. We anticipate that all traditional forms of communication will be shut down once the revolution kicks off.

This week we also had members around the country map out all the Rex 84 Camps. In 1970 there was a thesis written called "National Survival-Racial Imperative". This document was written by United States government official named Louis Giuffrada, who would later become president Ronald Reagan's FEMA director. This document went into specific details on procedures needed in order to lock the masses of Black citizens up in case of a large-scale rebellion. In the 1980's, under Ronald Reagan's presidency, this document was updated and amended, with the racial language removed, and given the name Rex 84. The government created several of these Rex 84 concentration camps all over the country in order to round up and contain large numbers of Black people at the opportune moment.

We are going to target these camps as well.

We have also linked up with members who are able to create prosthetic makeup. This is very important because we plan on hiding in plain sight. The prosthetic makeup is going to come in handy before the actual date of the revolution. Some of the members have worked in the film industry, and they know how to apply special effects makeup to a level where a person's real identity, and race is unrecognizable.

We also had Kelton Rose get all the addresses to the Negro collaborators with white supremacy. The white media will oftentimes put genuine Black sell-outs on their platforms to denigrate Black society on behalf of the white supremacists. They will also prop up Black sheriffs and Black police chiefs to do the dirty work for the white racists throughout the country.

In almost every major slave rebellion in history, there was often one common denominator. The slave rebels killed the Black collaborators first. This sent a message to the other rebels.

Serious missions call for serious policies.

JUNE 5th, 2079

W E HAVE RUN INTO A major problem. Today a federal agent came to my home asking me questions. Around 10:15 am this morning a white federal investigator named Robert Levitt showed up to my place and asked me if I was in contact with any "radical or militant" groups. I talked to him while standing in my doorway, and I had no intention of letting him into my home.

I pretended I didn't know what he was talking about when he was asking about possible radical organizations I was associated with. He told me, based on Intel, he had reason to suspect that I was possibly in contact with subversive groups. The conversation was very brief. It lasted about three minutes. I simply told him I don't know of any radical or subversive groups. I took his card and told him I would keep my eyes and ears open.

After the agent left, I immediately got online and started to look for any unusual activity from certain Nouvo Saracen members. Because we are less than a month away from the big day, and now we have a potential snitch on our hands.

And it can only be someone from a handful of people who know who I am.

I have made it a point to be anonymous, even with most of the Nouvo Saracen members. I do not give orders and strategies to most of our revolutionaries directly. I exchange information and tactics with a small group of comrades, and they trickle the information down to other members.

My mind is swirling a mile a minute trying to analyze the different angles here. There are a lot of unanswered questions I have. Who could have snitched? How much info do the feds have? If the feds have sufficient info about me, why wasn't I taken into custody? This is the thing that is confusing me. It doesn't add up.

But I'm going to find out who the informer is. Because it could only be one of six people:

Zedelph
Kelton Rose
David
Christopher Roy
Reverend Randal Prescott
Gerald Harris

So now I have to monitor the behavior of everyone to see what feels unusual with them. Because I'm going to get to the bottom of this. Aborting the mission is not an option. I also need to get some intel on that federal agent Robert Levitt. He' a 40-something Caucasian dude, who carries himself as if he had served in the armed forces. And I need to find out everything I can on this person. But my go-to research guy Kelton Rose could be the potential snitch.

I'm going to meet up with everyone this week, one by one. Meanwhile, I have to do a lot of planning, strategizing and researching on my own for the time being.

JUNE 7th, 2079

Today I have ordered more food and water to be stored in different safe houses around the country. I try to make large orders like this every week because once we kick off the revolution, we anticipate the white supremacists are going to implement martial law. So that's going to cause a major run on food and other essential items. So, we will be ready.

Earlier this afternoon, I met up with Kelton Rose. We were going through some training maneuvers and other details, and I went out of my way to speak at a minimum. I allowed him to do most of the talking because I was trying to pick up on his vibe to see if anything seemed suspicious. But based on our interaction, everything seemed normal with Kelton.

As we were talking, Kelton relayed to me how he and a few other Nouvo Saracen members arranged and pulled off the retaliation murder of a white race soldier employed as a police officer. A few days ago, a race soldier in Ohio shot and killed another unarmed Black 14-year-old child. And this child happened to be a relative of one of our Nouvo Saracen members.

Instead of getting extremely emotional, like so many of us do when we experience a racially based tragedy such as this, some of the local Saracen members in Ohio covertly set up a plan to ambush the officer. Kelton retrieved the address of the officer by researching information online. Once they got the officer's address, they faced two challenges: who are they going to get to pull off the hit? And how are they going to compensate the person who does the hit?

Somehow, they ended up getting Gerald Harris and Christopher Roy involved. Kelton contacted Gerald about ways to pull off the ambush hit because Gerald pulled off a similar ambush killing himself. So, when Kelton contacted Gerald about information on pulling off a covert killing like this, Gerald gladly assisted with as much information as possible. And Gerald also recommended some street dudes from one of the townships in Ohio to pull off the hit.

Once they established who the person pulling off the ambush killing would be, and how much he would be paid, Kelton and Gerald now needed to find out how they were going to get the money to the shooter. This is where Christopher Roy comes in.

Kelton hacked into a bank system and started funneling the money into a virtudigits account that Christopher set up. Virtudigits is a cryptocurrency similar to what Bitcoins were decades ago before the Bitcoin market crashed. Christopher was able to convert the virtudigits into cash without the source of the currency being revealed.

Christopher and David drove over to Ohio with the cash and untraceable guns that David secured to give to the designated shooter. Once they reached Ohio, they gave the shooter-a local street soldier- $12,000 cash and the weapons. The following day, the ambush was fairly simple. Kelton provided the shooter with the police officer's address, and the shooter camped out a few doors down from the officer's house early that morning. When the officer left his house to get in his car to head to work, the shooter simply drove up next to the officer's car and shot him six times, killing him instantly.

I fully condone ambush killings. Because the only way a marginalized, oppressed group can escape the tyranny of an empire, is to engage in guerrilla warfare tactics and ambush killings. But I think Kelton and the others should have waited before they did this mission. The big day is coming up, and none of us needed any type of extra heat coming our way. Because all the news outlets started covering the murder of the white officer on a 24 hr. cycle. So now law enforcement is shaking down Black people in every township in the state of Ohio, and in other cities around the country. They are basically harassing people until someone can provide pertinent information about the ambush murder.

As I'm listening to Kelton give about details of the ambush murder, I concluded that Kelton, Christopher, Dave, and Gerard were not involved in any kind of collaboration with law enforcement. The police would definitely not cut a deal with anyone who ambushed a cop.

So, the only other people who could have said something to the Feds about me is Reverend Randal Prescott and Zedelph.

JUNE 10th 2079

TODAY I MET UP WITH Zedelph at our usual spot at the cafe outside one of the townships. We were going to over our usual strategies and intel for the big day. I was also trying to read Zedelph' s non-verbal language to see if anything seemed suspicious about him.

As we were talking, he revealed that the FBI had visited him yesterday asking him questions about being a part of a subversive group. And he also got word that federal investigators paid a visit to Reverend Randal Prescott this morning. "We have a rat in our circle, Mike. And we need to expose who it is asap," Zedelph said. "I definitely agree, but who can it be?", I replied. "Because I was visited by a federal agent the other day."

Zedelph looked at me with a surprised expression. "Really? Why didn't you say anything about it?". "Well I didn't want to say anything until I could feel everyone out," I said. Zedelph thought quietly for a second. "Well it could only be someone from a short list people who could have tipped off the Feds," he said. "I know this. That's why

I quickly went around to all the other guys in our circle to feel them out."

I explained to Zedelph that only six of us have information that would lead investigators to each of us. And I also explained how I monitored some of the others and it simply doesn't make sense how anyone of them would be able to collaborate against us. Based on their circumstances, it just doesn't add up. Zedelph and I agreed to limit certain information to just the two of us for the time being.

We are still going to carry out this mission. We have come too far to be sidetracked at this point. As Zedelph and I were talking, he described the federal investigator that visited him. "When that agent showed up, I would not let him in my house. I just talked to him through the cracked door. When I first saw him on my security cam, I saw a tall, 40ish looking white dude, coming to my door? He has to be with the Feds."

I looked over at Zedelph and said, "wait, what's that agent's name?" He said, "I think his last name was Levitt." "That's the same agent who can visit me," I replied. "I wonder if he was the agent who visited Reverend Prescot?", Zedelph asked. "I gotta get to the bottom of this," I said.

Later on, today after my meeting with Zedelph, my mind was racing 100 miles a minute trying to sort out all the angles and possibilities on who the informant could be. I don't want to lose focus on the mission. So, I have to figure out ways to gather all the resources needed to execute the mission, while I'm keeping a close eye on everyone's actions within my circle.

It appears that many of us in the circle have been visited by the same federal agent. This suggests that there is no official investigation, just an ambitious agent trying to gather enough information to bring on a full-scale investigation. If the agent knew the extent of our plans, one of us or even all of us, would have been arrested already. Now if this Levitt guy keeps poking around, he is going to find something. And having our mission neutralized is not an option. I'm going to nip this investigation problem in the bud.

JUNE 12th, 2079

TODAY I MET UP WITH Kelton at his place. I still have no idea who in our circle gave information to the feds, and I'm still skeptical about disclosing too much information at the moment. But I have a certain level of trust for Kelton because he would be the least likely person to cooperate with law enforcement. I explained to Kelton that a federal agent visited me and some of the other inner circle Saracen members. I also explained that the federal agent probably doesn't know the full extent of our plans, and he is just trying to gather enough information to launch an official investigation at this point.

Kelton and I tried to brainstorm and figure out who in our circle was the informant. Then Kelton made a suggestion that seems like he was reading my mind: "What we need to do is snatch that federal agent up and make him tell us what we need to know," he said.

That was exactly what I was thinking. For years, Black people have been taught to fear law enforcement. That fear is just a holdover from being on slave plantations and being afraid of the white master or overseer. A great man once said the secret to life is to live with no fear. And we as Black people are going to stop having this fear of survival. Too many Black people have accepted this mindset where they are willing to sacrifice their survival so that the white supremacists can feel powerful. Those days are over.

I'm going to go and get that federal agent myself personally. Kelton looked through the deep web and found the information on agent Robert Levitt's home address. I'm going to have to do this mission myself because I don't know who to trust at this point.

After I snatch Levitt up and detain him, I'm going to need a secluded location to take him to. I don't want to take him to any of our meeting locations here in New York at the moment. Kelton recommended a storage facility that is located in the small town of Calvary Pines, which is a two-hour drive outside of New York City. That's one of the stash locations that Kelton and another Saracen member use to store weapons.

So, if I am going to bring a federal agent to one of our stash houses, I have to be very concise about this mission.

JUNE 16th, 2079

FOR THE LAST FEW DAYS, I went to the address that Kelton gave me for FBI agent Robert Levitt. I would go to his place and sit discreetly outside in an unregistered car that we obtained from an automobile chop shop near where I live. I staked out the house to learn his daily routine. I would go over to the area near his home in the late afternoon at first. But he would return home at different times, so it was difficult for me to assess his routine.

Yesterday I parked near his house at 6 in the morning to see if I could catch him leaving early. Sure enough at 7:10 am I saw him walk out of his house and to his car. I knew I had to act fast because I might not have another opportunity to catch him.

I already had my 9mm gun ready with a homemade flashlight noise suppressor attached to it, sitting on my passenger seat. I rolled my passenger window down, and I slowly began driving towards Levitt. As he was putting his coat and his briefcase in the backseat of his car, I drove up and shot him in the leg. He immediately fell to the ground and started screaming in pain,

I put the car in park, grabbed some duct tape from my backseat, got out, and ran up towards where he was lying on the ground. I have to move fast because I knew if he kept making loud noises, someone would be alerted. I tied the duct tape around his mouth, then I picked him up and quickly walked him to my car.

I opened the trunk, and I grabbed some handcuffs that I purchased at a surplus store yesterday. I put the handcuffs on Levitt; then I wrapped his leg with a shirt that was in the car to stop the bleeding, then I duck taped his ankles together. I put him in the trunk of the car, then I hopped in the driver's seat and quickly drove off. I headed for the interstate, and I drove directly to Calvary Pines.

I tried to drive as quickly as possible without risking getting pulled over. I didn't want Levitt to bleed out before I got all the information I needed from him. I finally arrived in Calvary Pines in about an hour and 45 minutes. Calvary Pines is an eerily quiet town that seems to consist of strip malls and a large fishing pond basically. That pond is going to come in handy, shortly.

I finally find the storage facility. Even though the facility is on an empty road and there are no people or other cars in sight, I still parked in the back of the building so I can remain discreet. I go to my duffle bag and retrieve the keys to the building that Kelton gave to me the other day. I opened the door, and I go in to take a look inside. The interior looked like a moderately sized warehouse with large shelves on the side. All the shelves were stocked up with hundreds of handguns, rifles, and shotguns.

After I saw that the coast was clear, I went to the car and brought Levitt inside. I sat him down in a chair that I moved to the middle of the floor. I removed the duct tape from his mouth. "You're never going to get away with this," Levitt said as he clenched his teeth and struggled to talk through the pain in his leg. "Federal agents are going to be all over your ass," he continued.

"Well, that's neither here nor there," I replied. "I just want to know one question. Who tipped you off about us?" Levitt looked up at me with an appalled expression. "You are out of your mind," he barked. "I'm not telling you a goddamned thing". At this point, I took out my gun, pointed it at Levitt's other leg, and without hesitation, I took one shot.

Pow!

When the bullet hit his leg, he screamed,"oh shit! What are you doing?"

While I still had the gun pointed at him, I said: "yes you are going to tell me what I need to know." Levitt was rocking back and forth in pain, while still trying to maintain a tough demeanor. "Go to hell," Levitt said while looking up and me with a sinister stare. I remained calm, and I let him know how serious I was about getting this information.

"Levitt, I'm going to shoot you in the arm if you don't tell me who snitched on us," I said as I moved closer to him. He sat there for a few seconds cringing in pain and breathing heavy without saying a word. I aimed my gun and shot him in the right arm.

Pow!

Levitt screamed as the bullet penetrated his arm. This time he was willing to talk.

"Ok, ok, look!", Levitt screamed, as he struggled to maintain consciousness. "Nobody snitched on you. There was a shooting in Ohio a few weeks ago where an officer was killed. Once the gunshot went off, sound monitors in the city located the area where the gunshot was. There are cameras around the city that film 24 hours a day, and we pulled up video logs of all the license plates on vehicles driven within a five-mile radius of where the gunshots rang out and the time it happened."

"Ok, but what does this have to do who snitched on me?" I said. "Like I told you, asshole, no one snitched on you", Levitt said as he was squirming in pain. "One of the license plates numbers we pulled up was for a vehicle registered to a man named Christopher Roy. Once I ran a background check on him, I saw evidence of large amounts of money sent to offshore accounts. And when I pulled up phone records, I saw that you and a couple of others were in constant contact with Roy," Levitt said.

I was temporarily stuck in deep thought at the moment. Christopher Roy must have let the shooter use his car to carry out the ambush killing of that race soldier. How in the world could he be that stupid to make a mistake like that? I tried to contain my frustration and focus on Levitt, and how I was going to handle him.

"What else do you and the bureau know about us?" I asked while still pointing my gun at Levitt. He sat up defiantly and said "We were just in the beginning stages of our investigation. But I can tell you now; you bastards are going to get the death penalty at this point. Harming me just sealed your fate. You and everyone you are associated with are going down. Doing any kind of harm to a federal agent carries major sentences. And once my colleagues see that I'm missing, they are going to be hunting for you today. So in other words, you are in deep shit Makandal."

I walked up to Levitt and pointed my gun directly to his head. I said "no Levitt, you don't understand. You all are the ones who are in deep shit. We are on a freedom or death mission. We have no problem dying to try to ensure our survival." Levitt looked up at me while trying to still maintain consciousness because he is bleeding profusely at this point. "Cut the Black nationalist crap. Sounds like you are just going to go out and get a bunch of people killed", Levitt said.

"Yea, many of us might die, Levitt," I said to him while still pointing my gun directly at his head. "But we are going to take as many of you out with us as possible. And I'm starting with you first." I pulled the trigger and shot Levitt in the head. His lifeless body dropped to the floor in one large thud. I got all the information I needed from him, so he was useless to me at this point. Most Black people in New Albion have been programmed to have a complete fear about harming someone employed as a law enforcement representative. Especially if that person is white. What many Black people fail to realize, is we are in a war. And this is a war of racial extermination. So Black people are going to have to learn how to fight back in this war and execute some of these race soldiers. And learn how to do it without emotion.

After I neutralized Levitt, I looked around the storage facility and found 3 large dingy covers. The covers looked like they were used to cover furniture or other items. I used two of the covers to wrap up Levitt's dead body. I used the other cover to wipe up the blood from the floor. I almost didn't care about Levitt's blood and his body being found. Because I know that this upcoming revolution is going to change society as we know it. But I didn't want any evidence found on the premises that could come back to haunt me before we got the revolution started.

After I finished wrapping up Detective Levitt's body in the covers, I tucked the other blood-soaked cover inside an opening within the wrapped covers by Levitt's feet. I went over to the back door and looked outside to see if the coast was clear. Once I saw that everything was clear, I went back in and quickly lifted Levitt up and carried him to the car.

After I put Levitt in the trunk, I went back to the storage facility to make sure everything looked ok, and I locked the doors after I left. I discreetly drove to the freeway and started heading towards that pond I spotted earlier. I got off the freeway and took a back road that led to an entrance to the pond. Even though it was the middle of the day, the area was empty, and there wasn't a person in sight. I pulled up to the bank of the pond. I looked around and made sure there were no hidden cameras or prying eyes. I saw that no one else was out there, I then went to the trunk, carried Officer Levitt's lifeless body to the bank of the pond, and I tossed him in.

I didn't bother to tie Levitt's body down with a heavy object. If he floats to the surface later on today, so be it. As long as I got him away from the storage facility, that's all that mattered. In the very near future, this entire system will be taken down. And there are going to be a lot more bodies floating around.

JUNE 20th, 2079

ODAY I PLAN ON GETTING some more metal containers in order to make some homemade pipe bombs. I got some new instruction manuals for explosives from Kelton when I went by his place two days ago. When I was there, I explained that officer Levitt informed me that he got all the information about us because Christopher Roy was careless. We then brainstormed on how we were going to handle the situation with Christopher. Even though Christopher is a great accountant and he is excellent at moving money, we simply can't afford to have another slip up like this one.

Kelton suggested an extreme solution. "If push comes to shove, we might just have to pop him," Kelton said as he made a hand signal that mimicked a shooting gun. I looked at him in shock. "Man, we can't do that. He didn't deliberately snitch on us", I said. "But if he's slippin' like that, then he's a weak link anyway. Right?" Kelton replied.

Yea he got caught out there slippin', and it could have been detrimental to our mission," I said. I continued, "But we need Christopher right now. He is one of the best money guys out there." Kelton quickly replied,"So what do you suggest we do about him, Michael?"

"I think we should send him to Eredo and have him post up over there and focus on getting the economic infrastructure in order," I said. Because the reality is, Christopher should not have been involved in an ambush killing at this stage, at all. And I think Kelton realized this eventually. Christopher is not built for that type of street business. So it would make sense that Christopher would slip up and not cover his tracks thoroughly.

So finally we agreed to have Christopher go over to Eredo this week because we don't know if there are other agents are tracking him over here. And we have to be careful because we don't know who else is tracking us. This is why we have to remain focused and try not to be sidetracked by other issues.

Kelton and I both spoke with Christopher on ham radio. We have to really take these types of precautions right now to make sure our conversations aren't being tapped. We explained the situation to him, and he understood that he has to go to Eredo right now. He was shocked and very apologetic when he found out that he inadvertently led the federal officer to us. We assured him everything was still good between us, and that it would be best for him to be in a position where he can just focus on the economic development.

After we nipped that business in the bud, we needed to check in on some of the Saracen members that we had infiltrate local law enforcement agencies around New Albion. Some of our plants gave us more Intel on the names and addresses of police officers and police union bosses who helped cover up cases of murder and brutality of Black citizens by police. They also provided names and addresses of the family members of these race soldiers. These lists are going to come in real handy in a few weeks.

JUNE 28ᵗʰ, 2079

RIGHT NOW THE NOUVO SARACENS are 300 deep all around the country. The members have been screened and vetted, and they are all ready to put in work. We have allocated resources to top Saracen members to recruit car thieves to assist us. We need experienced car thieves from townships all across New Albion to help secure a large number of stolen vehicles. And we need these car thieves to also teach other people in the townships how to steal automobiles. On the day of the revolution, these cars are going to be used as weapons.

Christopher Roy is set up over in the country of Eredo, and I have certain top-ranking Saracen members making sure that we send economic resources over there to him. Christopher seems to have quickly adjusted to the atmosphere over there, and he has no complaints.

On the home front, I got word from Zedelph that the government has devices called melanin sensors. These radar-type devices can detect and target people and areas that have significant amounts of melanin in the skin. After the melanin level is identified, they can then send gases that will specifically target and kill the person who is exposed to the gas.

Evidently, the government created these sensors in the case of a potential uprising from the Black population in the townships. So they have always anticipated an uprising against anti-Black non-justice. And they have tried to remain prepared at all times. As far as the melanin sensors, from the information I received from Zedelph, the only way to protect yourself is to use a specific type of sunblock with the chemical hydroquinone in it. So we made sure to spread the word to Saracen members around the country to secretly stock up on this sunblock.

This afternoon I bought 4 flamethrowers from a local hardware store. I have been telling the Saracen members all around the country to stock up on flamethrowers because they are going to come in handy. And they are easily available at any lawn care or hardware store. As I was driving home, I heard a news report on the radio that authorities discovered the body of federal agent Robert Levitt. The report went on to say, police are now launching a massive investigation to locate the perpetrators of his murder.

It's time for me to lay low until game day.

JULY 3rd, 2079

I HAVE BEEN STAYING IN MULTIPLE motels for the last week, using alternative identification documents provided to me by Kelton. There is a nationwide manhunt for the killer of federal agent Robert Levitt. I haven't had anyone investigating me so far, but I'm still going to stay mobile and move around as much as possible to be safe.

I put the word out to all the Saracens that they need to stock up on homemade bomb-making materials. Now, this can pose somewhat of an issue for Black people. Because the oppressor society goes on alert when they see Black people purchasing large quantities of over-the-counter items that can be weaponized. So I told everyone to go to their local hardware stores and pay some immigrant day laborers who are usually posted up outside of these stores looking for work, to buy sodium chlorate so it won't be suspicious. If some Mexican day laborer purchases the items, the people in the store will simply assume he is using it for gardening or something of that nature.

Some of the Saracen members who are military vets have been teaching other members survival and combat techniques. Many of the members complained about the training, saying it was too strenuous. But this type of training is exactly what we need to get out of that comfort zone. We have to set aside that comfort zone. Hogs are in comfortable settings before they are slaughtered. And these white supremacists plan on slaughtering us in large numbers. So we need to be in survival mode 24 hours a day.

This week, Kelton also set up some hologram streaming websites, using servers from other countries. We did this so when we start documenting and broadcasting the events during the revolution. This way, the New Albion government won't be able to shut down the stream easily.

The good thing about hologram streaming is if a person has a certain phone device, they can access your hologram stream. And a low-resolution digital stream of yourself will appear on their device. We are going to need all of this as a means to communicate when the Revolution is in full swing.

The white supremacists are used to Black people rioting and taking their frustrations out by attacking objects. This time is not about destroying property. It's going to be about stacking up the largest body count possible. Either we will eradicate white supremacy, or they are going to eradicate us.

· ·

JULY 7th, 2079

W E ARE ONE WEEK AWAY from the big day. I have set up a meeting with myself and other top-ranking Nouvo Saracen members to take place this week in St. Louis. I need to go over some strategies and objectives with these members.

News media reports are showing that law enforcement is turning up the heat on the investigation into agent Levitt's murder. Police have been shaking up random Black people in townships all over the country. Race soldiers have been aggressively harassing and arresting large numbers of Black people in hopes that they can get someone to talk and give up information. Yesterday, in one of the local townships, police were looking for a potential suspect, and a white police officer ended up shooting and killing an innocent 20-year-old Black man. And because this shooting is already linked to another high profile investigation-the murder of federal agent Robert Levitt- the police shooting of the 20-year-old is getting a lot of national press coverage today.

Judging from interactions on social media platforms online, there is a lot of tension brewing across townships all over the country. Many Black people are getting angry that they are being targeted because of the Levitt murder. This is actually a blessing in disguise. Because once we get the revolution starts next week, we can use this collective frustration and anger from Black people in townships around the country, to galvanize them into action and joining segments of the revolution.

We are still getting money from the churches across New Albion. And we are still funneling that money to our allies in African nations. Christopher Roy is still over in Eredo, and we are sending some of our qualified people over there to work him. Some of the people we sent to Eredo are engineers who are helping to create nuclear weapons to protect some of the counties there from white supremacist terrorism.

Today we also sent out certain Saracen members to plant explosives in key locations around the country. We sent our prosthetic make-up people around the country to do disguises for the Saracen members. These particular members were made up to look like elderly white people. Some were made up to look like homeless white people. This allowed them to go into white populated areas around the country and not raise suspicions.

Initially, we were going to hire some white drug addicts to plant explosives for us. But too many people in white society abide by a code of white supremacy, and they will look out for each other, in most cases. And we don't have the time or the luxury to try and figure out what white person is not on the white supremacist code. So using prosthetic make-up on Black people who was down with our cause, was the only practical option at this point. And it worked.

We had Saracen members plant explosives outside of malls, airports, train stations, courthouses, and other places where large numbers of people are known to occupy in these communities that support and enable racial injustices. They also planted explosive near some of the Rex 84 centers around the country.

I have to get packed and ready to fly out to St. Louis tomorrow afternoon for the meeting this week, and I have to check in with Zedelph and Kelton. I need to make sure that they had everyone attending the meeting this week thoroughly screened. We cannot take any chances with potential infidels or turncoats in our mix. The dawn of the revolution is here, and everything must go off without a hitch.

JULY 10th 2079

'M IN ST. LOUIS RIGHT now, on my last day here. I'm driving back to New York tomorrow. I chose to drive down here because media reports are showing that the manhunt for the killer of federal agent Robert Levitt is intensifying. I didn't want to take any planes or other public transportation methods to get down here, at the risk of potentially being caught.

We had the meeting down here yesterday with the other top-ranking Nouvo Saracen members. We had the meeting at a warehouse owned by one of these members down here. The warehouse also acts as a safe house to stockpile some of our weapons and ammunition. There were approximately 50 members present at this meeting. This was the first time all of us met in person face to face. We took time to screen each member who was present thoroughly. We even had private investigators do surveillance on each of these attendees to make sure they checked out.

After we counted all the people who were supposed to be in attendance, I then took to the floor. The speech I gave to the attendees went straight to the point:

"Gentlemen, we are here today to discuss the most important event to ever happen for Black people. We are going to make a large scale offensive strike against the white supremacists. The last time this was done, it happened centuries ago in Haiti. And their revolution was successful. But they did not have a complete follow up plan. And we do. We have allies in other countries who we are working with to set up stable economic systems. We also have scientists, and military experts in these countries working with our allies to set up large-scale defense mechanisms that will enable us to protect the economic system we set up."

"Gentlemen, we will not be like the Tasmanians, full-blooded Native Americans, Australian Aborigines ,German Jews and others, who sat around waiting for their extermination at the hands of white supremacists. We are going to fight back for our survival. The creator did not put us melanin-rich people on the planet to be destroyed by an evil system of white supremacy."

"That is why it is up to us melanated people to destroy this system. We must understand that this revolution means freedom or death. There will be no in-between. And we must not fear death. Complete liberation is worth dying for. There is no honor in living like an insect-completely subjugated under the white supremacists."

"For centuries Black people globally have chosen to live in fear under the white supremacists. many of us have failed to realize that the secret of life is to live without fear. And we Nouvo Saracens have chosen to be completely fearless in the face of systematic white supremacy."

"Again, the secret to life is to live with no fear. That is the purest definition of freedom. In four days we are going to take our freedom. There is no freedom under the system of white supremacy. This is why we have to dismantle that system completely."

"We have tried to negotiate with the white supremacists. But that never really works out in the long run. We are basically prolonging our subjugation. There is no negotiating with white supremacists. Historically, the white supremacists have reneged on every deal they have ever made with non-white people. There is no honor among white supremacists. They only value domination. And we must value our survival."

"So you do not have to have a sense of honor when it comes to defeating the white supremacists. That type of logic only makes sense when your opponent values honor and integrity. When you are dealing with an opponent who doesn't value honor, there are no moral rules of engagement when defeating them. You have to win by any means necessary. So if we have to be deceptive, manipulative, or even unfair when it comes to defeating the white supremacists, so be it. We have to win or die. There is no in between at this point."

"We have all been training to master the art of guerrilla warfare tactics. We will not make the mistakes that other Black people have made went going up against the white supremacists. Black people's approach to white supremacy has always been reactionary. And the reaction is usually filled with emotion. And that has always been the biggest mistake. As a rebel soldier, you have to be as logical and strategic as possible."

"For years Black people have made the mistake of only destroying property whenever they have rebelled against racial injustice. This is usually an attention seeking tactic. Deep down, many Black people are comfortable living under the system of white oppression. And they want to throw a few objects around in order to let their white masters know that they should ease up on the mistreatment a little bit."

"We are not going to go that route. Our objective is to kill as many white supremacists and suspected white supremacists as possible. And we will engage in property damage for the sole purpose of solidifying the destruction of the white supremacist system. We care not about seeking attention from the white supremacists or showing off in front of news cameras. We have to focus on stacking up bodies."

"Once we get the Revolution started, we have to be very cognizant of the retaliation from the white supremacists. They are going to come at us with their greatest strength. Their machines and technology. This is why we avoid the machines. For decades, Black people have engaged in the process of throwing rocks and objects at the tanks and armored vehicles used by the white supremacists. This has always been an ineffective, time-wasting maneuver on the part of Black people."

Throughout history, the white supremacists' greatest strength has been their machines. And their greatest weakness is them without their machines. This is why we have to focus on attacking the white supremacists in situations where they do not have their machines to back them up. We are going to attack them in places where they are comfortable and relaxed. We are going to their homes and their communities. Avoid the machines at all costs. We must concentrate our efforts on ambush attacks, and surprise hits. We have to operate like ninjas. The key to our success is stealth. We have to hit the enemy in their weak spots. This will initiate and gradual and progressive takedown of the white supremacist system."

"Understand, once we start the Revolution, we cannot stop until there is a victory. Once we get started, there will be only one of two outcomes: Our complete genocide or our complete success. There is no in between."

"We are going to make public examples out of Black people who collaborate with the white supremacists to keep us subjugated. We are going to publicly execute them live online. We will do this so that any potential Black collaborator will understand the consequences of selling out Black society."

"We Nouvo Saracens do not fear death. And this is going to be our greatest strength. Because if we die, we have sacrificed our lives for a worthy cause. And that is more honorable than living like a subjugated insect, waiting on someone to exterminate you. We are engaging in this battle so our next generation can survive. So once the battle starts, we do not surrender. If we are in a situation where one of us is facing guaranteed death, the objective is to take as many people out along with you as possible."

"This will also be the first time that Black people took a preemptive strike against white supremacy. We have always been reactionary when it comes to dealing with the white supremacists. And this is why we have historically lost against white supremacy. The only time in recent history where Black people initiated a battle against the white supremacists was in the Haitian Revolution. That's one of the reasons that is the most successful revolt by Black people."

"So, Gentlemen, we are now ready to do what Black people should have done a long time ago. Stomp out systematic white supremacy by force."

At the end of my speech, the men in the room gave a round of applause. The atmosphere among the group was now exciting and intense. Everyone was even more motivated and eager to start our mission. I let people know that we should make sure that all loose ends, if any, were covered in the next couple of days. We wrapped up the meeting and prepared to head back to our individual cities.

In a few days, history will be made. 300 rebel soldiers are going to wage war on the mightiest country in the world.

JULY 13th, 2079

THIS MORNING I GOT UP bright and early and went to a local hardware store to buy some extra gas-powered generators. As I passed the appliance section in the store, one of the display televisions was showing a newscast. I glanced at the television set, but I wasn't really paying attention to what the people on the tube were talking about. My mind was on getting all the supplies I needed on time.

Suddenly, I see an image of myself through my peripheral. I turn my head towards the television, and I see a news anchor mention my name and I see a DVM photo of me on the top right of the screen. The news anchor said, «surveillance videos led authorities to a vehicle registered to a New York man named Michael Makandal. He is wanted for questioning in the vicious murder of federal agent Robert Levitt.»

At this point, I had to quickly leave the store before anyone could recognize me from the news report. I abandoned all the items I was going to purchase, I lowered my head, and walked as fast as I could to my car. Now that law enforcement is on my trail, I cannot go back to my apartment at this point. I sat in my car for a moment to figure out what my next move would be. Luckily, I already ditched the vehicle I used to take agent Levitt to the lake, weeks ago. I was now driving an untraceable vehicle from a chop shop owned by a Saracen member. So I didn't have to worry about my vehicle being spotted.

I decided to head over to Zedelph's place. I called him from one of the throwaway cell phones I had, to let him know I was on my way there. When I spoke to him, he told me he saw the news reports, and he was trying to reach me as well. The big day is tomorrow, and the last thing I need right now is to be captured and confined. Law enforcement agents are most likely on their way to my place right now, if they haven't been there already.

Once I reached Zedelph's place, I went inside, and we discussed strategies and tactics on how I could lay low until tomorrow. Luckily, I have only corresponded with all of my Saracen comrades through ham radio or untraceable "burner" phones. So it was fairly safe to reach out to other comrades and remain undetected by outside entities. We reached out to one of our members who had a safe house/ weapons armory not too far from here. We decided that would be the safest place for me to go and post up until tomorrow.

Zedelph gave me two of his guns that he had stashed at his place, and I prepared to head out to go to the safe house. On my way out the door, I looked over at the television in Zedelph's living room, and the news was showing footage of my apartment being raided.

The only thing they are going to find in the apartment is large containers of freeze-dried food and water bottles.

I made sure to move out any evidence of the upcoming rebellion that was stored at my place a few weeks ago. I did it as a way of playing it safe until the day of the rebellion. And it appears my gamble was worth it.

All of my weapons and supplies were stored at another safe house, located 45 minutes outside of the city. I wish I could go directly to that location, but with my face plastered all over the news, and the fact that it's still morning time here, someone could easily spot me in traffic. So I left Zedelph's place, got in my car and started driving through side streets towards the safe house near this location. I called my comrade who owns the safe house, which is basically a small unmarked, freestanding office building, and he told me he left a key near the side entrance of the facility.

It took me almost two hours to get to the safe house. Taking all those side streets took up most of the drive time. Once I got to the safe house facility, I parked a half block away. I walked up to the side of the building and looked around for the key. I saw a small stone trash bin sitting outside the building. The entrance key was sitting in the ashtray part of the trash bin.

I got the key and went inside the facility. The safe house was a large office space with two smaller side rooms. The office was packed with weapons, packs of dried food, bottles of water and small solar-powered generators. Thankfully, I have everything here I need to be ready for the big day tomorrow. The only two downsides are one; I have no access to the internet right now at this facility. And two, I don't have access to my own bed where I can be nice and well rested for tomorrow.

I go in one of the smaller rooms and find a narrow

sleeping area with a twin size bed and a dresser table. There is a small solar powered am/fm radio on the dresser. I picked the radio up and turned it on as I climbed onto the bed to lay down. I searched for talk news stations, and I eventually stumbled upon one station discussing the manhunt out for me. The news report said there was now a reward for my capture. The report went on to say that not only was law enforcement looking for me but deputized militia groups were looking for me as well.

I turned the radio off, and I laid on the bed for a while thinking to myself: The white supremacists are looking for me. And tomorrow morning they are going to get what they are looking for and then some.

. . . .

JULY 14th, 2079
REVOLUTION TIME

8:00 am EST

I WAKE UP IN THE SAFE house. I had a good night's rest. So now I'm fully charged. The first thing I did was get on my burner phone and make sure some of the other Saracen members were in position.

We are going to launch simultaneous attack all over the country. We are going to launch the first strikes at 10:00 am est. The Saracen members on the West Coast are going to strike at 7:00 am their time. The members in the central part of the country are going to strike simultaneously in their time zone.

We are setting our ham radios to the same frequency so that we can correspond with each other. You generally need a license to operate a ham radio. But today we are not worried about the laws of New Albion. Today, we are going to be the law.

10:00 am Est.

Fires are set on buildings simultaneously all over the country. By setting multiple fires on properties in major cities, the emergency phone lines are jammed up. We specifically make sure that fires are set in certain white supremacists neighborhoods that have a history of supporting race soldiers.

We also launched simultaneously ambush attacks on white supremacist race soldiers working as police officers who have been acquitted of harming Black people. I personally drove over to the home of a race soldier here in the New York area and set his house on fire. When he came out of the house with his wife, I shot both of them and killed them. Other Saracen members were doing these types of ambushes in multiple cities as well.

We carried out the same type of ambush killings against police chiefs and police union presidents as well.

10:10 am EST

We rounded up groups of known Black collaborators of white supremacy. The Black people are considered the coons, mammies, and bed wenches in our society.

We simultaneously executed the Black sellouts and we make sure all the killings were videotaped. We then post the videos online.

We anticipated that SWAT teams were going to be deployed. So we had Saracen members around the country go to different SWAT headquarters and start fires on the buildings and do ambush shootings on the officers who exited the premises.

10:15 am EST

Saracen members all over the country proceed to freeway overpasses in specific areas where large numbers of white supremacists and suspected white supremacists reside. I go to one myself here in New York. We throw spike strips onto the freeway from the overpass areas. Multiple cars blow out their tires driving over the spikes. As the traffic starts to jam up, we pull out semi-automatic weapons and start mowing down people in as many cars as we can. This causes further pandemonium and major traffic jams all over the country.

At the same time, Saracen members in big rigged trucks drove up to different prisons all over the country. Once they get outside of the prisons, the Saracen soldiers opened up the back of the truck, and rolled out small construction tractors. Some of the trucks in certain cities contained small cranes with wrecking balls attached. Once the members rolled the tractors and cranes out of the trucks, they began to tear down parts of the outer walls of the prisons. Thousand of prisoners started immediately fleeing from the facilities. All the prison guards who came outside, were immediately shot down with machine guns. The Saracen members didn't get all the prisoners out, but they helped to release a significant number of inmates, and that's going to help us build our army.

10:20 am EST

Saracen members around the country round up and kidnap white supremacist jury members who sat on high profile cases where race soldiers were acquitted of murdering Black people. Kelton Rose hacked different courthouse databases and compiled a list of all the names. We are going to make an example of these white supremacist jury members by executing them live on streaming video later. We are going to take all the kidnapped white supremacists to hidden locations within the townships around the country. We are going to use some of them and their children as leverage later on.

Some of the drug dealers we have recruited for the revolution are helping us to dispatch a number of their drug using customers. The dealers are giving the users small quantities of free foam to smoke, and they are promising larger quantities after they complete certain tasks for us. We are having the drug users spread throughout the cities into white supremacist areas and throw bottles of cocktail bombs into crowded business areas.

Other Saracen members around the country are continuing to set multiple fires on homes and businesses in white supremacist neighborhoods. Several members go into shopping mall areas and airports around the country. These are the few places where a large number of suspected white supremacists would congregate in the morning on a weekday. Once the Saracen members arrived at these locations, they immediately pulled out their semi-automatic weapons and started killing large numbers of suspected white supremacists. There were bodies dropping and people scattering through pools of blood everywhere. This is a very unfortunate necessity. This is war and warfare is not pretty. This is about survival. Either they are going to kills us, or we have to kill them. We made a choice to kill them. This is business not personal.

10:25 am EST

We started strategically setting off bombs that were placed near significant areas around the country. Some of these areas included National Guard centers. We knew that the National Guard would be deployed immediately after the start of the revolution. So we wanted to strike them early so they could be caught off guard. We knew that this would cause a sense of paranoia among troops in the National Guard. We also destroyed many of the Rex 84 internment camps that were set up all over the country. We used homemade bombs to destroy the facilities partially, and we used cars to ram down the gates and fences. These acts will compromise the white supremacist's ability to detain large groups of people in their camps.

Saracen members around the country go to the homes and job locations of known white supremacist judges and prosecutors and ambush them on sight. Many of these judicial figures are murdered immediately by Saracen snipers. These are the people who helped to maintain the racial system of non-justice, and now they are receiving karma for their deeds.

10:30 am EST

Emergency sirens start going off in locations all over the country. The New Albion government is now informing the public that the country is under attack. Television and radio stations are now warning the public of the attacks. There is complete confusion and pandemonium around the country at this point. Now that I know that law enforcement will be occupied dealing with the chaos caused by this rebellion, the coast is clear for me to quickly go back to my apartment to pick up some things I need. As I get to my apartment to quickly gather my necessities, my television is still on from yesterday, and I glance at the news reports. Reporters and officials on the news channels are trying to figure out who is responsible for these attacks. Pundits are speculating it could be Muslim terrorist groups. Some are speculating that it could be far East Asian countries that are hostile to the New Albion government, that are responsible.

The news pundits start to report that all the alleged suspects from the attacks around the country are Black. Once these claims are validated by several witnesses and surveillance cameras set up in public places around the country, the mass hysteria is intensified. This is the moment that the white supremacists on this continent have feared for centuries. The Blacks are engaging in a mass, coordinated revolt against them.

10:45 am EST

I leave my apartment, and I proceed across town to another safe house that also doubles as a vehicle warehouse. As I'm driving I see traffic is backed up, loud sirens are going off, and there are clouds of smoke covering the sky. In this city alone, the entire area has been thrown into anarchy by only a small handful of Saracen members. I'm looking for some side streets to take in order to get around these traffic jams. As I see an empty one-way street up ahead, I notice in front of me there are three police cars with their sirens on, stuck in traffic. I reach into my backseat and dig into my duffle bag. I pull out one of my Semi automatic rifles. I slowly drive up next to the three police cars and roll down my window. I opened fire on all three vehicles, killing everyone one of the white officers.

The people in the cars on the road heard the gunshots, and they started to panic. The began smashing into each other trying to get away. I quickly turned down the one-way street and took some alternate routes to the destination. It took me around 20 minutes to reach the warehouse. Once there, I went to the back of the building in a large gated area. There was a chain lock on the gate, and I had the key already, so I unlocked the gate and went to my solar powered RV that was parked near the back fence.

Now that I have reached my RV, it will act as a central command station for the revolution. I made sure to load the RV up with the most modern technology, weapons, and other resources. I have portable televisions, radios, and several internet and satellite cards to get online and communicate.

11:30 am EST

All the media outlets in the country are now reporting that there is an armed Black domestic terrorist attack occurring nationwide. Emergency sirens are ringing on almost every city block, it seems. News stations are reporting that thousands of white citizens have been killed in mass coordinated terror attacks. Local police agencies have been given orders to lock down all the Black townships in their cities until the National Guard can be deployed.

Riot police show up to townships around the country and tell the local Black occupants they must go inside their homes because martial law is now being imposed. Naturally, many of the Black citizens objected to the police orders. In one city, Miami, people started throwing rocks and bottles at the police officers. The police then brought in the K-9 unit, so that the dogs could attack the township occupants.

Many of the occupants were protesting and yelling at the police. We had many Saracen members secretly planted in some of these townships. And when the local police showed up with their K-9 unit, the Saracen members and some of their township affiliates released dozens of pit bulls onto the cops. All of the police dogs were instantly mauled to death by the pit bulls. As the pit bulls started attacking the police officers, the cops started panicking and randomly shooting at the dogs. Many of the officers were shooting each other during all the confusion.

Saracen members then started throwing a swarm of Molotov cocktails at the police and setting them, and their police cars on fire. While all this was happening, other Saracen members were sniping down police officers from windows and rooftops. The police were completely unprepared for this type of quick retaliation, and they hastily retreated.

This same type of scenario played out in dozens of other major cities in New Albion. Hundreds of race soldiers employed as police officers were killed and wounded within a matter of minutes and they were forced to retreat. Now we are fully aware that law enforcement is going to retaliate with a vengeance. But the good thing is, word has quickly spread around the townships that a Black Revolutionary organization is bringing heat to the police. And this has immediately granted us hundreds of new recruits. And these new recruits are fully on board with helping us increase the death toll of white supremacists.

12:15 pm EST

During all the confusion and mayhem around the country, some of the Saracen members in Miami dispatched boats to go down to Haiti and bring in reinforcements. The boats should be back later tonight. Other Saracen members around the country, myself included, went to the downtown areas of most of the major cities around New Albion that has a history of enabling Black subjugation. We brought out our flamethrowers. We started setting fires to as many businesses as possible. In some cities, the flamethrowers were used on suspected white supremacists civilians. Many buildings in these downtown areas are flame resistant on the outside. For these structures, we busted out the windows and threw Molotov cocktails inside the buildings to set them on fire.

We don't want to waste too much time burning random downtown businesses. The reason why we are targeting some of these structures is because we want to quickly sabotage the main business areas so that it will have a trickle-down effect on the overall economy in general. Our main objective is to get the white supremacist death toll up as high as possible.

12:30 pm EST

The New Albion government has declared martial law. They have stopped all flights and all other forms of mass public transportation. They are instructing all people to get out of the streets and go into their homes. Even though every media outlet is instructing the public to follow the martial law orders, people are still in the streets panicking all over the country. Mass hysteria and mass confusion has taken over nationwide. The National Guard and private, government-funded military groups have been dispatched to go lock down all the townships around the country. Armed white militia groups have taken to the streets, and they are ambushing random Black people who are in the areas close to the townships. Once people in the townships see that there is this retaliatory pushback from the white supremacists, this creates more recruits for us.

There are many Black people who are trying to distance themselves from the revolution. Many Black people are being interviewed on media outlets, crying about "peace" and praying for all the white victims. Many Black people around the country are gathering in churches at the moment in an attempt to show submission. Many Black people are even going out of their way to help and assist the white supremacists. We have learned how to use that Black cowardice and submission to our advantage. Some Saracen members will pretend to help the white supremacists by posing as all-forgiving Negro Christians. But we capture many of the white supremacists. And some of them are taken to different hiding places within the townships, while others are captured and killed on the spot.

We started setting fires to several gas stations around the country, and this caused numerous major explosions. Several people were killed in these blasts that were predominantly set off in white supremacist residential areas. These explosions also caused more major fires around the country as well.

12:45 pm EST

Many race soldiers are at the townships around the country in full riot gear. Authorities are trying to clear off the freeways in order to bring in armored vehicles. But because of the massive traffic jams, this task is almost impossible at the moment. Many of the riot police have to form human walls at this point as a way to show force in the townships. This was something we anticipated. We deliberately wanted to get the streets and freeways jammed up so that it would be more difficult for the white supremacists to bring in their machines. We are trying to create maximum damage while we have this major window of opportunity.

While the police were surrounding the townships in an armed formation, several Saracen members proceeded to use stolen cars as weapons. The members got into these vehicles and began to speed toward the line of officers, running them over and killing several of them. Many of the officers tried shooting at the vehicles. Some Saracen members got killed during this process. But several more suspected race soldiers were killed using this tactic.

Word got around throughout other townships around the country that we are using cars as weapons. So everyone began stealing cars and using them to mow down people in suspected white supremacist areas. We killed thousands of white supremacists in a short period of time, using this tactic alone.

While all this nationwide confusion is going on, we sent Saracen members to certain white supremacists areas to poison the water supply. This immediately took effect, and people started dying in droves. Saracen members are continuing to set fires in these areas as well.

I'm getting reports that certain Black people who live in the township areas were surrendering to the white supremacists. From what I understand, hundreds of Black people were taken to local jails and immediately killed upon arrival. This let other Black people know that surrendering at this point was no longer an option. They are going to have to join the fight, or die.

1pm EST

The New Albion government has finally mobilized their tanks and machinery to reach the townships around the country. They immediately started setting off and utilizing their advanced weapons. The government has developed a Melanin Ray. These are large satellite dish looking weapons that emit rays that specifically targets skin melanin cells. Once a person with a high dosage of melanin comes in contact with these rays, they immediately become paralyzed. And some people die from exposure to the rays. The National Guard used these melanin rays on thousands of Black people in the townships. Black people started dying instantly. The ones who didn't die and were just paralyzed, rounded up and incarcerated.

Many of the Saracen members and their associates who were prepared for this type of retaliation, started to apply large quantities of sunscreen to become immune to the melanin ray weapons. We also got the word out to other Black citizens to use these sunscreens to protect themselves.

1:15 pm EST

Many of the national news outlets are scrambling to get their Black collaborators on television to denounce the violence. One of the top-rated so-called conservative news networks brought in Gerald Harris to speak out against the retaliatory Black on white supremacy rebellion.

The live broadcast took place at the news station headquarters in New York. For years, this particular news network has been responsible for a lot of anti-Black propaganda that is used to justify harming and killing many of the Black citizens in the townships. Gerald let us know what time he was going to be at the station. Several other Saracen members and I went to the area where the news studio was and discreetly posted up outside. There was still a lot of pandemonium going on outside in the streets, so we will barely got noticed anyway.

We watched the live broadcast inside of my RV. The news program went live, and the anchor, a popular suspected white supremacist, named Bob Miller, introduced Gerald Harris. Bob Miller is known to bring in Black people to regurgitate his anti-Black talking points so that he can hide his racism behind these Black pundits. "The entire nation of New Albion is under attack," said Bob Miller as he stared into the camera. "Hordes of Black savages are roaming the streets of our country right now, causing complete terror and mayhem." We have one of our most popular guest returning on the program, Gerald Harris to chime in."

The camera cut to a close-up of Gerald. Bob Miller continued, "Gerald, what do you think about the way these degenerate thugs have gone on the warpath?" Gerald looked at Bob, and put in right hand inside of his coat and pulled out a pistol. Bob was paralyzed with shock and fear. Without saying a word, Gerald pulled the trigger and shot Bob Miller in the head at point-blank range on live tv.

You could hear the camera and production crew in the background scattering and screaming. Gerald walked out of frame, and you could hear several more gunshots in the background before the live in-studio feed was cut off and interrupted by a commercial.

At this point, other Saracen members and I went inside the lobby of the television network, and we started shooting everyone in there. There was one Black janitor that we spared. But we wiped out everyone else there and made sure Gerald got out of the building safely.

This was a very important move. Because now, the white supremacists can no longer trust their Black collaborators. This makes the white supremacists more paranoid and desperate. And when people are paranoid and desperate, they are more vulnerable and prone to mistakes. Because paranoia and desperation trigger emotions. And emotional decisions during wartime is a bad combination.

1:30 pm EST

During all of the confusion, many dark-skinned, non-Black people were targeted by white supremacists in retaliation. Many East Indian, and Middle Eastern people were attacked by white vigilante groups. The white supremacists could not differentiate between these groups and black New Albion citizens. Nor did they care to.

Many of these dark-skinned foreigners were immediately killed. This caused riffs between the government of New Albion and the home counties of the slain immigrants. Some of these other countries started to plan attacks on New Albion as retaliation. We are going to use this to our advantage as well.

Many Saracen members started setting off homemade bombs at several white supremacist owned television and radio stations. We tried to kill as many on-air personalities and staff as possible. They have acted as the propaganda arm of systematic white supremacy. So they will be made an example of.

Other Saracen members around the country started to raid gun stores, which are mostly owned by suspected white supremacists. They quickly went into these stores and ambushed the owners by immediately killing them and any other customers who were in the stores. They then collected as many guns and ammunition as possible. Many of the weapons the Saracen members took were used to give to the newly freed former convicts who we helped to get out of prison. Once these brothers were armed, they were determined to fight the white supremacists to the death. Because they knew the only other option for them was life in prison.

And prison is not an option for any of us at this point.

1:45 pm EST

I have an untraceable cell phone, and I'm about to stream live from a hidden proxy web address that we set up months ago. I go to one of our safe houses where we have a number of race soldiers held hostage. Earlier, some of the Saracen members kidnapped six police officers around the city, blindfolded and handcuffed them, then brought them to the safe house.

We shuffled the race soldiers into one of the back rooms. I started broadcasting live on my phone. I looked into the camera and said: "Greetings everyone, my name is Mr. M. The rebels and I have now taken over the streets of New Albion." "We are responsible for everything that is happening right now. We demand that authorities around the country release every Black person from all the local jails." "We have already assisted in the release of several Black, federal and state prisoners."

"If Black inmates are not released from local jails within the next 45 minutes, more of this is going to happen."

I then turned the camera to the six-race soldiers huddled in the corner, blindfolded with their hands bound. I pulled out a 9mm gun and shot each of them in the head at point-blank range, killing them instantly.

I looked back into the camera and said "this is to show you that we mean business. You have 45 minutes." I then stopped the live broadcast. When I signed off, the video was automatically uploaded to our website. I called Kelton and had him share the website link of the video on social media sites. Within minutes, the video started to go viral. It's getting hundreds of thousands of views within minutes. The media immediately picks up on the video and air it nationwide.

The video sends terror throughout the nation. The visual of white race soldiers being executed for war crimes against Black citizens by Black citizens is one of the greatest fears of the white supremacists.

Race soldiers posing as police officers represents security and maintenance of racial non-justice in the white supremacist system. And their job is to implement fear in the minds of Black citizens so that we will bow down and accept the racial mistreatment of the society at large. But now that fear is gone. And we are bringing the fight to the race soldiers. And the rest of white supremacist society understand that we are coming for them now in full force.

2pm EST

We are continuing to use the scorched Earth tactic of burning down everything we possibly can to the ground all over the country. Fire is our chief weapon at the moment. We are using Molotov cocktails, flamethrowers, and other fire starting mechanisms to torch buildings and homes in white supremacists communities.

The media has reported that the stock market is essentially crashing before our eyes. People are starting to make runs on the bank, despite the martial law orders. As millions of people line up at banks around the country to withdraw their money in the suspected white supremacist communities, Saracen members ambush these people and kill thousands.

In the timespan of just 4 hours, we have managed to kill an estimated 10,000 people. And we have almost destroyed the economy in the strongest nation on the planet.

Other enemy nations see that the country of New Albion is wounded right now. Even though the New Albion press is trying to have a media blackout of many of the events that are happening at the moment, the international press is transmitting the revolution in full graphic detail. There were already members of the international media in New Albion doing other broadcasting assignments. And when the revolution got started they patched into the satellite feeds of the media in their own countries. The international community sees that new Albion is being destroyed from within. Now some other nations are going to use this as an opportunity to assist in the destruction.

Zedelph used some of his military connections overseas

to have the nation of Qatar get more advanced weapons to us. Over the last decade, Qatar has had strained diplomatic relationships with New Albion. And the fact that some Qatar nationalists were some of the people killed by white supremacists and race soldiers today, Qatar is ready to take action.

Zedelph arranged for the Qatar government to fly in weapons to Haiti. The weapons will include grenades and rocket launchers. Once the weapons are flown into Haiti, we will then have them shipped to New Albion by boat.

2:15 pm EST

We have made it a point to engage in nonstop attacks all over the country today. It is complete anarchy in the streets of New Albion right now. Even Black, non-Saracen members are randomly killing white supremacists in the thousands at this point.

The New Albion government has deployed almost every sector of their National Guard units. There are also several private military companies deploying troops around the country. The streets in all the major cities are now flooded with military personnel, armored vehicles, and other large-scale advanced weapons. We are still avoiding these machines at all costs.

The government has set up military units in all the Black populated townships around the country at this point. They also have military units set up in several wealthy white communities as well, in order to protect the inhabitants and the properties.

If the military is posted up in one part of a city, we make it a point to go set fires on the other side of town. We have to be as mobile and evasive as possible. There were Black people, who were non-Saracen members, in some of the townships who were trying to play the "throw rocks at tanks" game, but they were quickly shot down by the National Guard. They are learning quickly, that this is not a protest this is a war.

We executed more captured race soldiers on live video. While we are making these videos, we are very careful to conceal our identities. Even though law enforcement was already looking for me before the revolution, I still don't want to make myself a target at this point.

We continued to target the homes of well known white nationalists as well. This sent a message that none of the backup law enforcement militia groups are safe at this point.

The Government is now starting to strictly enforce the martial law orders that were implemented today. They have completely suspended the New Albion constitution, and they have set up checkpoints on roadways and neighborhoods all around the country. They are now rounding up and arresting random civilians who they deem "suspicious," without probable cause. This is going to work in our favor.

Now that Black citizens see that they no longer have the illusion of rights they are waking up and turning against the New Albion government in large numbers. This has immediately garnered us tens of thousand new supporters who are ready to join the revolution.

2:30 pm EST

The government has now deployed large fleets of fighter jets all over the country. Historically, air strikes have always been a stronghold tactic for the white supremacists. And this has been a major advantage for them when it comes to warfare. But even with the advantage of aerial weapons, you still need a target to use these weapons on. And at this point, they don't have one. The Saracens are basically invisible. Other than the videos I made taking credit for the uprisings while disguised, we have not made ourselves known publicly. That's our advantage.

The fighter jets are flying over townships around the country looking for hostile forces. And while they are distracted with targeting innocent people in those locations, Saracen members are ambushing other areas. In cities where there are subway stations, one of our most effective hit and run tactics is to set fire to a neighborhood or shoot down a large group of people, then disappear underground. This way we could avoid being seen or followed by the fighter jets.

Now it's time for our disguises to come in handy. We are using some of the "white" prosthetic make-up that we had created for some of the Saracen members. Some of the comrades have applied prosthetic make-up and they are now disguised as elderly white people. Now they can creep into certain communities to plant explosives without being detected.

While wearing these disguises, certain Saracen members slip into different areas and plant explosives on prominent bridges, railroads and at more airports. The timers are set to detonate an hour after installation to give each Saracen member ample time to escape.

2:45 pm EST

Thousands of Black people are being rounded up at the moment. The military is transporting them to some of the Rex 84 camps that are still functioning. Saracen members get the word out to each other through ham radio, on the locations of these concentration camps.

We dispatched units to some of these camps. We set up ambush teams on the roads leading to these facilities. When trucks rolled up with large cargos of Black people, we launched surprise attacks on the race soldiers.

We shot at the drivers of the vehicles, and killed several of them. When the transport vehicles came to a crashing stop, we opened up the back section where people were detained. We freed as many people as possible.

We distributed maps to other Saracen members, of underground sewer systems around the country. We obtained this info because there are several different Saracen associates who work in city planning positions. Whenever we plant bombs in certain neighborhoods, we immediately retreat to the underground sewer system. This way we can avoid being spotted by the fighter jets.

Once underground, we use flashlights to run through the sewer systems to designated pothole openings that have getaway vehicles nearby. We have to continue to be mindful to avoid the machines at all costs.

Some of our Saracen members who are in the armed

forces start launching attacks on other white people within the military. Across the country, they kill thousands of fellow "officers" who are suspected of being white supremacists. Immediately afterward, they went awol. This sent the entire New Albion military into a tailspin. They don't know who to trust.

Same thing with the local police. Saracen members have infiltrated law enforcement agencies around the country. So when large groups of riot police marched through different townships, some of our undercover Saracen members who are in their police uniforms, start spraying the officers with bullets.

In the area I was in, I parked my RV and took one of my machine guns out into the streets with me while I ambushed suspected race soldiers. I shot and killed an officer in a vehicle as he was about to turn a corner to drive down the street. After I shot him, I pushed him into the back seat. I jumped behind the steering wheel and proceeded to drive off in the police car. I headed towards one of the townships where riot police were scattering away from being fired upon.

I started picking off random officers I saw running down the street away from the other officers. There were three other suspected white supremacist race soldiers running down a side alleyway. I proceeded to follow them in the police vehicle. As I sped up behind them, I see that the alley leads to a dead end. Once the officers realized they were trapped, I quickly pointed my 9mm handgun out the window and shot all three of the race soldiers in the head.

When I prepared to back out of the alley, a police car pulled up with two officers. They parked directly behind me, and the officer in the driver's seat jumped out and aimed his weapon at me.

"Hold it right there and don't move!", the tall white officer screamed at me. I turned around in the car and started shooting through the back window. As the glass shattered, I could see the officer fall to the ground. Two of my bullets caught him right in the head.

The second officer ducked down behind the side of the police car. He started shooting at me. I ducked my head down under the steering wheel in order to dodge the bullets. When I got back up, I tried to shoot back, but I couldn't get a solid aim on him while he was hiding behind the car.

As I ducked back down, I started revving the car engine. I put the gear in reverse, and I backed up and crashed into the officer's vehicle. I continued to press my foot all the way on the gas pedal so that I could push the officer's car into the wall of a building behind him. Once the officer jumped from behind the vehicle, I then opened fire on him, striking him in his head and neck, killing him instantly.

This was a close call for me, so now I have to focus on more strategic ambush attacks, that won't end up in close call scenarios like this.

3pm EST

Law enforcement and the military are currently occupied with the thousands of Black people who are looting stores for television sets and clothing. The New Albion government has now put the country in full lockdown mode. They have just issued an executive order to stop allowing people into the country. They have also issued an order to stop people from leaving the country as well. They want to keep everyone potentially involved with the revolution locked down and detained.

The Saracens have made an oath not to surrender or allow ourselves to be detained. We fight to the death. Either the white supremacists die, or we die.

While law enforcement and the media is occupied with the activities of looters, Saracen members have kidnapped more white suspected race soldiers occupied as police officers and put them in one of our many secret stash houses. Several other Saracen members are executing these kidnapped race soldiers live on streaming video so the world can see how serious we are. We want the public to know what this revolution is about. This tactic is helping us recruit even more members by the thousands.

All the new members joining forces with us are all given one basic instruction up front. Burn down everything you can in suspected white supremacists neighborhoods. There are currently tens of thousands of fires all over the country right now. With all the bravado the New Albion government tries to display to the international community, the government was ill prepared for an event like the revolution that is taking place.

In less than six hours, we have completely destabilized almost every facet of society in New Albion. And the day is not even over yet.

3:30 pm EST

The bombs that we have timed to detonate in multiple locations just went off. The explosives we planted has destroyed parts of freeway systems and other areas that facilitate transportation. The bombs also took out bridges and other transportation means.

Certain areas are now inaccessible for military and emergency vehicles to enter from the ground. This is why we made sure to have Saracen members start several fires in these areas and get out of the vicinity as quickly as possible before the explosions went off. We did not want any of our comrades getting trapped in these areas.

Helicopter units have been deployed to these areas to help put out the several fires that were started. We are going to use this as a distraction to go into other neighborhoods and attack more water and power supply units.

Pipe bombs we planted has blown up dozens of structures around the country and killed thousands of people. This has driven people to more pandemonium.

While the general public is distracted and confused, Saracen members are securing more weapons and food supplies from empty gun shops and grocery stores around the country. Also, we are ambushing government run entities that are holding the gold reserves. Many of the people who guard these sites have been deployed to duty in other areas around the country. They have been directed to go to the townships to fight who the government calls insurgents.

This has placed the gold reserves in a vulnerable position because now they don't have the proper manpower guarding the facilities.

Several dozen Saracen members, including many new recruits, stormed one particular gold reserve located in the outskirts of Atlanta. They used a bulldozer to bust into the facility. They immediately shot down several employees. They left a couple of the guards and employees alive. They used these employees to help them gain access to the gold vaults.

Our comrades ended up taking mass quantities of gold that were worth millions of dollars. Several guards at other gold reserve facilities were killed by Saracen members in a similar manner during the process of us securing the gold.

4pm EST

Several more white supremacist militia groups have started to roam around the country and shoot every Black person they spot. These groups have basically been deputized by the government and law enforcement.

The word has quickly spread around the townships that these militia groups are further targeting Black people, so we have recruited more rebels to ambush them on site.

Other Saracen associates went to police stations around the country and bombed as many police vehicles as possible outside of the stations. We are also ambushing every police car that is spotted. We are still staying clear of the armored military vehicles.

Many Saracen members around the country are still using flamethrowers to attack race soldiers who are wearing armored gear that bullets cannot penetrate. The fire from the flamethrowers has proved to be very effective in neutralizing the race soldiers in armor.

Many of the Saracens are going to Ohio to stock up on the cache of weapons we have stored in the multiple safe houses we have there. They are going to distribute the weapons to other rebel fighters in their cities.

Emergency sirens are still going off all around the country non-stop. Even though martial law is implemented and no one is supposed to be out in the streets, there are so many neighborhoods on fire, many people have no choice.

Since New Albion is a member of NATO, other allied nations are starting to gear up to assist the government against the rebellion. This is something we anticipated. This is why we set up many sleeper cells in these allied nations.

The military of Greece was about to deploy assistance to New Albion, so we had Saracen members in Greece set off similar guerrilla warfare attacks there as well. We did this same tactic in a number of other allied countries as well. This caused these nations to have to redirect their focus on calming the social mayhem in their own societies and securing their own borders.

Our attacks have set off the beginning of what could be a World War.

4:30pm EST

We have Saracen members who are pilots, secure private airplanes at smaller airports that were not attack. We have some of our comrades fly the gold that we took from some of the reserves out of the country. The cargo was flown to Brazil, and from there it will be flown to Eredo Africa.

Right now there are military fighter jets flying all over New Albion. But without a designated target, they are not effective against our constant guerrilla attacks. We are unleashing a constant barrage of firebombings, ambush shootings, car attacks, and explosive detonations. And law enforcement has no idea who to target. Their dragnet tactic of rounding up every Black citizen has completely backfired on them. This has created more recruits for us. And we have more attacks planed into the night.

Many of our Saracen members who are in the military are launching more ambush attacks against the suspected white supremacist soldiers within their ranks. This has caused more terror and paranoia within the armed forces across the country. Some of these Saracen members have secured military tanks, and now we are using those weapons against the New Albion government.

There have been 7 armed military tanks that have been hijacked by militarily trained Saracen members around the country. We have used those tanks to wipe out hundreds of riot police and suspected white supremacist civilians. These tanks are also used to level several buildings and structures in certain cities. These tanks are also used to free more Black prisoners who are locked up in correctional facilities around New Albion.

We don't want to make ourselves targets by utilizing these armored military vehicles over a long period of time. So we have to use the tanks for very fast and strategic attacks that will have a maximum impact. So we must make sure we hit large groups of race soldiers when we strike. And we have also used these tanks to shoot down some of the aerial military units that are flying over these cities.

We have to really get prepared to deal with these air strikes against the Black citizens of New Albion. Because the white supremacists understand that they have already lost the ground war against us. In less than a 12-hour time span, we have neutralized thousands of white supremacists, we have destroyed trillions of dollars in property, we have destabilized the New Albion economy, and the government and the military don't even know who we are. They are familiar with me and a few other rebels, but they have no real grasp of who to target in order to thwart the rebellion.

5:00pm EST

Reverend Prescott has been contacted by the media to come out publicly and denounce the revolution. The media has been reaching out to Black preachers all over the country to get them to help quell the attacks.

Many of these preachers have declined because we have targeted Black people who appeared to be in collaboration with the white supremacists. But Reverend Prescott is our guy, so him agreeing to work with the media and law enforcement was part of our plan.

The reverend agreed to have an emergency press conference and mass prayer service with people from the suspected white supremacist community and members of his congregation. This gathering is scheduled to happen in a couple of hours.

5:30pm EST

We now have Saracen members targeting shipping ports all around the country. Rebels are going to sabotage the New Albion trade and supply lines as much possible today. Saracen members started setting fires to shipping ports and the storage containers around the areas. Rebels also shot holes into several ships, sinking many of them in the process. Some rebels even killed several crew members on some of these supply ships. The word quickly reached many of New Albion's trade partners, that shipping supplies to this country is dangerous.

We also had rebels who were trained in the Navy, assist in securing some of the ships and boats from many of the ports we have seized and convert them into makeshift warships for the Saracens. We made sure these impromptu warships were heavily armed, and our rebels used them to patrol the trade ports and ocean borders around the country.

Saracen members have to do their best to avoid the New Albion Navy's battleships from coming into contact with them. The only time they are supposed to engage the Navy is when they are doing ambush attacks against them.

More military personnel has been dispatched to patrol the cities and try to calm the chaos. In some areas, police officers have been killed, and their dead corpses have ropes tied around their neck. They are then hung over from the rooftops of buildings so the media outlets can see.

The images of white police officers hanging by their necks from the top of buildings is devastating to the public. There is a media blackout at the moment, where the news is deliberately going out of their way not to show images of white supremacists being killed by rebels. So now, several civilians are filming these images and putting them online, making them immediately go viral.

All the images of executed race soldiers and suspected white supremacist circulating online have made more Black citizens who want to join the revolution.

As more riot police and military are being dispatched to the townships around the country, we are now prepared to use our store-bought drones to launch air attacks.

6:30 pm EST

Military and law enforcement around the country are having a difficult time trying to protect white supremacist communities and lock down the townships at the same time. We are continuing to exploit this weakness by continuing non-stop ambush attacks on white supremacist occupied suburbs and race soldiers.

Since many of the race soldiers were dispatched to be concentrated in large numbers near the townships, we came up with efficient ways to ambush the enemy. We used our ham radios to communicate with Saracen members around the country to coordinate the next ambush strikes. We told Saracen members to make sure they posted up in proximity to the areas near the townships, but not too close to be in jeopardy of getting caught.

Once we were posted in these areas, we then placed homemade explosives onto the drones. We set 45-second timers on the explosives before they were released. We flew the drones with the attached explosives over crowds of police officers. We then dropped the drones into the crowds of officers right before the explosives were detonated. Once the explosives went off, dozens of officers were killed instantly.

There were still several air units of law enforcement and military hovering over the cities. We directed Saracen members to use the drones to attack these air units as well. Once we observed air fighters that were hovering low enough, we quickly released the drones and explosives up near these aircraft. Many of the drones missed their mark, but there were still several aircraft that were struck taken down.

The military tried to scramble the signals of our drones, but Kelton gave everyone into on how to put a special kind of magnetic strip inside a certain section of the drones so they wouldn't get affected.

This sent a message and a sense of fear to the military. They now became more cautious with their air patrol strategies.

7:30 pm EST

Now that it is nightfall around the country, our revolutionary attacks will now become more intensified. We had Saracen members around the country attack power grids in different cities. This shut off the electricity and many major cities were in complete darkness at this point.

The marching orders to Saracens and our thousands of new recruits was to go into white supremacist neighborhoods and burn down everything in sight. And all the people trying to escape the burning areas, kill as many of them as possible.

In the cover of darkness, rebels all over the country stole vehicles, broke into gun stores to stock up on more ammo, and raided grocery stores to stock up on more food and water.

The Black people who took to the streets to loot stores for trivial clothing and electronics items like televisions and speakers, inadvertently provided an excellent distraction for the real rebels. While law-enforcement and white supremacist militia groups were swooping down on the looters, the rebels were further destroying the white supremacist communities and neighborhoods.

Also, while law enforcement and the military was busy rounding up and neutralizing the looters, security at the ports and harbors was becoming weaker. The military is still using the Melanin Ray weapons to kill thousands of Black citizens. These Melanin Rays are also killing many dark-skinned non-Blacks who are immigrants. Many rebels are broadcasting these killings live on the Internet for the international community to see.

These mass executions are further agitating the home countries of many of the immigrants who are being targeted by the New Albion government. After video footage was streamed online showing a group of dark-skinned Iranian immigrants being killed by New Albion military soldiers, the Iranian government launched an attack on New Albion. The Iranian military launched a ballistics missile towards New Albion. The missile landed in the middle of the country, destroying parts of Wyoming, Nebraska, Iowa and South Dakota.

The New Albion military started to gear up for a counterattack against Iran. Some of our comrades working within the military informed us that three different military facilities that house nuclear warheads were getting prepared for the counter strike . These facilities were located in Nova Scotia, Chicago, and Orlando. We used our ham radios to galvanize Saracen members in those areas quickly.

We instructed our comrades inside the military to keep us abreast on what was happening with the planned counterattack. As soon as we received the proper intel, Saracen members and other newly recruited rebels attacked these facilities. The Black military members who pretended to be patriotic to the needs of the government, assisted Saracen members with taking over these facilities. They gave the rebels pass-codes and outlines of these facilities so they could gain access to the nuclear weapons.

Once inside these facilities, Saracen members quickly murdered every suspected white supremacist military personnel staff member on the spot. They then used the codes given to us by our military members to override the systems and get to the nuclear warheads. Saracen member took high ranking military personnel hostage and tortured them until they gave the rebels additional information on utilizing the warheads.

We have now successfully taken control of three nuclear weapons from the New Albion government in three different locations around the country. This is a game changer.

8:00pm EST

Thousands of people crammed into Reverend Prescott's church for the emergency press conference/prayer vigil. The majority of the people there were white, and there were many people from the media streaming the meeting live on television.

The reverend went to the podium and addressed the crowd and the media with the typical "we have to stop this violence and come together under the name of Jesus" speech. He then invited several white people in attendance, who were from surrounding communities to step up to the podium and give their testimonies.

Many of these people were explaining that they were not racist, and they have Black friends and that they understand why Black people would be upset over police brutality, etc.

But these were the same people from these suspected white supremacist communities who got on juries and allowed race soldiers to get away with murdering innocent Black people. They knew this was wrong, yet they were still complicit. So it's too late to own up to the injustices now. The power of punishment is now in our hands.

While the different white people were lining up around the podium to speak one at a time, Reverend Prescott slowly eased away from the pulpit area into the back chambers. There was so much focus on the emotions and hysteria of the attendees, no one even noticed the reverend creeping out of the venue.

About five minutes after Reverend Prescott was cleared from the church venue, armed Saracen members walked out onto the balcony area of the church. They then proceeded to shoot and kill every non-Black person who was in attendance.

8:30pm EST

Now that we have leverage against the white supremacists with the nuclear weapons, we are now going to take over some of the media airwaves. We dispatch masked Saracen members to some of the major news networks around the country. We let the media know that they better give us immediate air time or we will send these warheads to white supremacist cities all over the country. The media got word from New Albion government officials to not allow us on the air. The government wanted to test us to see what we were fully capable of.

We had our military Saracen infiltrators launch one of the smaller nuclear warheads towards Northwest New Albion. It's landed in an area that was formerly known as North British Columbia. The impact and explosion of the warhead destroyed 2 states in that area. These areas were fully segregated white supremacist enclaves, so millions of people were instantly wiped out.

This let them know that we were not bluffing by any stretch of the imagination.

Armed Saracen members finally went into multiple television broadcasting companies and forced the staff to put them on air. The rebels were still wearing masks when they appeared on air informing the public that this was not a coup taking place. This is a full-on revolution, and it's racially based.

Zedelph appeared on one of the live channels wearing a mask as well. He informed the public that there had been a government takeover. He also announced that every remaining Black prisoner incarcerated in New Albion should be released within the next 30 minutes. If not more white supremacists are going to die. Before he could continue, the live broadcast was quickly shut off. The FCC headquarters in Washington DC interrupted the broadcast and shut it down.

We put our message out just in time. We were fully prepared to carry out our next series of nationwide ambush attacks on white supremacist civilians. But moments after our broadcasted message, radio stations were interrupted with an announcement from the government that all of the Black prisoners are being released immediately.

In warfare, one has to be very careful not to back the opponent too far into a corner. That will create a scenario for them where they have to fight for survival. We are creating an option where our enemies will want to fight to escape our wrath.

About 15 minutes after the government's announcement, all the federal prisoners in New Albion were released. 90% of all the federal prisoners in New Albion were Black. And when the government released the prisoners, they included the 10% of other races of people.

I wasn't too pleased with this. Many of these other non-white groups have allied themselves with the white supremacists. None of these other racial groups lifted a finger to help the Black people of New Albion. And these same groups are sitting on the sidelines during this revolution.

They are waiting around to see what kind of residual results they can parlay into tangibles for their groups.

So when we kick the door of freedom open, we are not going to let them run in next to us. They have put in work like the Black rebels of New Albion are putting in work now. If they don't, we will not allow them to align themselves with us, because they will end up sabotaging our efforts.

9:30 pm EST

Some of the Saracen rebels who took courses on how to fly planes and other aircraft, have stolen police helicopters all over the country. The rebels are using these helicopters to fly around the city and drop homemade bombs.

The boat from Haiti has arrived in Miami. Another one of our boats from Cuba arrived 25 minutes ago. The boat from Haiti has 50 rocket launchers and anti-aircraft weaponry, along with 900 Haitian men and women squeezed in.

The boat from Cuba has 1200 Black Cubans who are ready to put in work for our revolution. We arranged to have several buses waiting on the Haitian and Cuban rebel fighters to take them to safe houses around the Miami and southern Florida area. We are going to arrange for many of them to be dispatched to other cities around the country.

We also had big trucks waiting at the docks so we could load up the rocket launchers and other ammunition from the boats. Once loaded, Saracen members proceeded to drive off to different safe house locations around the country.

Some Saracen members are going to take time to get

in some rest. There is so much fear and anarchy happening right in the streets of New Albion, we are going to use this to our advantage.

Many rebels went to rural farm areas around the country to post up and hide out. These were ideal areas, because most of the inhabitants in these areas live on huge acres of land and they rarely interact with large numbers of people on a daily basis. So once the Saracen members went into these farm areas, and killed the suspected white supremacists owners, we understood that it would be a while before anyone noticed the absence of these people. So our rebels can stay in these areas for a significant amount of time without being detected.

Meanwhile, in other parts of the country, the Black rebels who are not directly connected to the Saracens are out in the street rioting, and many of the main Saracens rebels were getting much-needed rest.

THREE DAYS LATER: JULY 17th, 2079

7am EST

THIS IS THE THIRD DAY of the revolution. I and all the other high ranking Saracen members have been laying low over the past 3 days. Cities around the country are still burning. Martial Law is still in effect, but millions of people are roaming the streets trying to gain access to any resources they can find.

The New Albion military is out in full force. There are fighter jets flying all over the major cities around the country still. The Saracens are going into the next stage of the revolution. We are going to concentrate our much of energy on two cities: New York and Washington DC. These places are the political and economic headquarters of New Albion. We are going to topple many of these oppressive institutions that have systematically impacted Black citizens in a negative way.

We started targeting the families of local and state

elected officials. Several Saracen members converged on the homes of many of the lawmakers and government officials. We tried to kill as many of these government officials and their family members as possible.

We turned off the electricity in specific white supremacist neighborhoods by burning down multiple grids. Once the power was off, we were able to scale the walls of some of the gated homes many of these officials lived in without tripping the security sensors. We then set fires to these homes. Once the people inside started running outside for safety, we started to shoot them down, one by one.

This has created more chaos and destabilization of the government. Other countries are planning on launching more missiles toward New Albion. The government is in a real quagmire at the moment. They are dealing with foreign *and* domestic attacks. This has always been one of their greatest fears about Black citizens. Black people on this land linking up with foreign enemies. The New Albion government is draining all their resources with non-stop military occupation.

Several of the Haitian rebels that we brought in have been dispatched around the country. We have also strategically placed our rocket launchers in different cities around the country as well.

The New Albion government has started launching more air strikes in Black populated areas. They dropped bombs on multiple townships, killing thousands of Black citizens instantly. The government is now on a full out genocide campaign. This has garnered us more recruits.

We put the word out on ham radio to other Saracen

members to use our rocket launchers on these New Albion air units that were carrying out the attacks.

We transported some of the rocket launchers to Saracen members in Minneapolis. From there, some of them drove over to South Dakota with a very specific mission: destroy the faces on Mt. Rushmore.

Once the Saracen members reached Mt. Rushmore National Park, they started live streaming over the Internet. We wanted to makes sure the entire world had a chance to see someone destroy the major symbols of white supremacy.

Our rebel soldiers fired the rocket launchers at the mountain and blew off the faces of George Washington, Thomas Jefferson, Theodore Roosevelt, and Abraham Lincoln. After the smoke cleared, the stone monuments became unrecognizable. This was the first time, on this soil, a major symbol of white supremacy was toppled and destroyed by Black citizens.

After seeing this, the white supremacists are now ready to fight to the death. And for the first time in the history of this country, so are we.

8am EST

We used some of the suspected white supremacist hostages to negotiate the release of more Black people who were incarcerated in city and local jails around the country. We let officials know that we were ready to start executing the white hostages who were former jury members, including their children, if all the Black county jail inmates around the country were not released within 20 minutes.

White city officials immediately released the Black inmates, and we freed a few of the white hostages in return. Part of warfare is letting your opponent feel like they have an exit strategy. When people feel like they have no exit strategy, they will fight to the death. But if you allow them a small exit strategy, they will concentrate their energy on making an escape.

9am EST

Saracen members around the country used large trucks that were stolen from multiple sources, to barge their way into local zoos. The rebels continued to break down fences and barriers inside the zoos in order to free the animals.

Rebels used wooden planks to place in the animal sanctuaries to allow the wild breasts to escape. Certain glass enclosures were shot out so that more animals could escape. We made sure that the most predatory and dangerous animals were released. The rebels released lions, tigers, gorillas, elephants, alligators, hippos, bears, and every other type of dangerous animal.

The rebels made sure to hurry back to the safety of their trucks once the animals were released. The reason why we ordered Saracen members to release these animals, is because we are going to use them as weapons.

Most of the zoo facilities around the country are far away from the township areas. So once these animals escape, they are going to pose a further threat to the white supremacists communities that are near the zoo areas.

10am EST

There are live news reports of some Saracen associate's names being broadcasted on television. My name is included on this list. The authorities did some investigating, and they started to locate many of our identities. We anticipated this.

When the authorities went out to raid our homes, we already had the locations booby-trapped. When the police officers arrived, different types of explosives went off, killing many suspected race soldiers in the process.

As the military continued to hover around townships in helicopters and other aircraft, we coordinated a strike against the race soldiers. We used the ham radios to give orders to Saracen members all over the country to use the rocket launchers to shoot down the government's helicopters and military aircraft. And these attacks are instructed to launch tonight between 10:15 and 10:30 am pst.

We also instructed rebel fighters to use their handguns and assault rifles to shoot down some of these aircraft as well. I'm still posted up in New York monitoring all the nationwide activity in my RV. At this point, we have initiated a total collapse of order in the New Albion society. The military is essentially trying to restore order. And we are going to do everything to make sure that doesn't happen on their terms.

10:30am PST

Saracen members and our rebel allies launch simultaneous attacks on military helicopters around the country. Rebels shoot off rocket launchers that immediately blow up and destroy military aircraft that are flying over townships. The rebels who do not have access to the rocket launchers, fire their guns, and assault weapons at the helicopters and military planes, taking many of them down in the process.

We also have more Saracen members who have infiltrated the air force. Many of them take control of fighter jets and start using them against other military compounds. They also shot down many other military jets flown by suspected white supremacist soldiers.

These actions caused further mistrust among people in the military. Consequently, this has caused the military to become somewhat destabilized in their plans and actions. This has made them more vulnerable to the attacks that are being launched against New Albion from other countries.

12pm EST

There are more emergency warnings in the media warning the citizens of New Albion that there is a missile headed our way from another Middle Eastern country. There are also emergency sirens going off in the streets around the country.

Many of the military fighter jets and aircraft are now being used to fly overseas and deal with the international threat. Now that the military powers have been weakened, we rebels are going to go full scorched Earth right now. We are going to go into more areas and destroy the land.

We are setting fires to huge farmlands and agriculture

areas. The New Albion government is powerless to stop this because they have no idea who to specifically target. And their tactic of targeting all the Black citizens of New Albion has backfired on them because this is creating more rebel fighters.

At one of the townships in Chicago, the New Albion military is flying helicopters over the area, and they are shooting down any Black persons they see outside. Because there was martial law declared, every Black person was considered fair game to be killed by the military because just their very presence outside was considered "breaking the law."

We just so happened to have a number of highly trained Saracen members posted up in this particular township. One of the apartments in this township was being used as a holding area for white supremacist hostages and race soldiers who were kidnapped in that area.

Some turn-coat Black person in the area must have tipped off law enforcement to the whereabouts of the hostages. We were prepared for situations like this in our various holding spots. The rebels started to implement a pre-planned getaway strategy.

While helicopters were hovering outside, the rebels got on their ham radios and alerted other Saracen members who were near the area. These other members were told to come to the township and repeatedly drive around the 5 city blocks that made up this township.

About 7 minutes later, several of the rebels came to the township and started driving around each block, as a way to distract the helicopters above. The Saracen member inside the particular apartment unit started to light up smoke bombs on the roof of the building. Other Saracen members and our allies did the same thing on several other buildings in the township.

The smoke from the smoke bombs clouded the visibility of the buildings, and the helicopters above could not see what was going on. Some of the cars that were circling around the township came in and picked up some of the Saracen rebels as they covertly slipped out of the building that held the hostages.

These rebels evacuated from the township, and once the smoke cleared, the military started throwing grenades inside the building that held the hostages. They then launched a direct attack on the building. They started shooting rounds of ammunition into the building and ended up killing all of the hostages.

12:30pm EST

There have been multiple animal attacks on people in the white supremacist communities around the county. We have been monitoring reports on police scanners, and there have been a plethora of calls stating that people have been mauled by wild animals from the zoos.

This has created even more pandemonium. And now the authorities are forced to exhaust more of their resources and manpower in an effort to contain the rebellion as well as the animal attacks. This is going to make the New Albion authorities more weak and vulnerable. They were completely unprepared for these types of surprise attacks.

1pm EST

The New Albion government has given orders to law enforcement and military all over the country to launch a full-on extermination attack against Black citizens. The government no longer wants to take hostages. The military has been instructed to kill Black citizens on sight. And the government has deployed more military helicopters to carry out this mission.

We are already prepared for these air strikes. We had Saracen members around the country pick up sewer pipes from hardware stores. We obtained wires, gunpowder, and other devices to create home-made rocket launchers to use against the air strikes.

These air strikes are the final resort of the white supremacist government. We have already defeated them on the ground. We have taken control of all the shipping ports and all of the shipping cargo. We have taken the fight to the white supremacists. So they are off balance right now.

The rebels around the country proceeded to set up their homemade rocket launchers. We sent messages and instructions to Saracen members on ham radios across the country to immediately launch attacks on the helicopters and planes.

As our counter-attacks were initiated, several military helicopters from the New Albion government were immediately destroyed. Right around the same time we launched these attacks, the missiles from a Middle Eastern country landed and destroyed several states in lower New Albion.

Around 2 million people were killed in that missile

strike. Unfortunately, around 10,000 of the people killed were Black people. But we understand that some members of a certain group will be sacrificed when it comes to warfare.

Millions of Black people around the country are starting to spread out and away from the townships at this point. Even the Black non-combatants are getting on-board with the revolution. We try to warn as many people as possible to still take major and minor precautions wherever they move around.

Unfortunately, many Black people have a habit of getting too comfortable and letting their guards down once they feel they are in a comfortable situation. Several Black people were venturing into many of these outside areas without sunblock on, even after higher ranking Saracen members warned them to.

Without warning, the government started using their melanin sensors to detect the presence of Black people in these outside areas. They then released ethnic gas that specifically targets certain levels of melanin. Thousands of Black people who did not have on the specified sunscreen, died immediately.

This was a major setback for the revolution, but it gave all the other Black people a clearer understanding of how important it is to stay on-code and listen to pertinent instructions.

2pm EST

Our next line of attack will be to target wealthy white supremacist gated communities around the country. Many of these elite white supremacists have insulated themselves in exclusive gated communities right on the outskirts of the major metropolitan cities.

We have coordinated these attacks like many of the other offensive strikes we have made. We used our ham and satellite radios to set up simultaneous attacks on these neighborhoods. We saved these locations for last because these are the people who basically run the country through economics and other think tanks that control policies. We also knew that these people are going to be the most heavily protected in the country. So now that we have essentially destabilized and in many instances neutralized their protection base-meaning law enforcement and the military-this group of people are easy pickings.

Saracen members arrived at these gated communities, and the first orders were to knock out all of the electrical grids near these areas. Living in these gated areas turned out to be a gift and a curse for these white supremacists. For years they were able to use their societal and physical gates to keep the non-white "threat" out. Now that society has broken down, and now that we have cut off their electricity, the gates cannot open, therefore they can't escape. So now their gated communities have become prisons. But this will not be a long incarceration.

After the electricity was cut, Saracen members climbed over the gates and proceeded to shower the homes in these areas with molotov cocktail bombs. In some cities, there was some exchange of gunfire with a few private security and military firms the people hired to protect their homes. There were a few minor injuries that some of our Saracen members suffered, but we were quickly able to contain, and neutralize these threats.

We have very specific orders for this last series of attacks: Kill every single white supremacist who lives in these areas. After we set almost all the homes on fire, there was a mad scramble for people to run out of their homes and escape the gated communities. But because the gates were locked shut and couldn't be opened in most of these areas, there were traffic jams of people trying to escape.

Saracen members started to shoot down these people in their cars trying to escape. People who tried to run and jump over the gates were shot down as well. Even though a small handful of these white supremacists did manage to escape in certain cities, we managed to kill the majority of the people living in these areas.

4pm EST

After we neutralized the elite white supremacists and after the missiles from the Middle Eastern countries destroyed significant parts of the Southern region of New Albion, Saracen members staged a coup against the military. The armed forces have become so divided and destabilized, we were now able to take over complete control of the military.

We took control over most of the weapons. The suspected white supremacist armed forces personnel who were not killed, were taken into custody. We sent most of these suspected white supremacist prisoners of war to one of our main detention centers on the Southern coast of Florida. We named this detention center The Camp of the Saints.

Saracen members who infiltrated the military, also helped us secure control over all the nuclear and advanced weaponry. We had to make sure we quickly gained control over all the advanced defense weapons before another nation with shared hostilities against the former New Albion regime launched an invasion.

Our allies in Eredo made sure to have nuclear weapons directed at any suspicious nation in Europe, the Middle East or Asia that may try to launch an invasion on the former New Albion nation. We also have sleeper cells in these countries who we trained and prepared to launch terror attacks if any of these nations decided to intervene against us setting up our new regime.

4 DAYS LATER:
JULY 21ˢᵗ, 2079

8am EST

THE NOUVO SARACENS HAVE SUCCESSFULLY overthrown the New Albion government. We have renamed the country Melantis.

We have now assumed complete control of the nation's television and radio airwaves. We have propped up Zedelph as the official leader of the new regime. We decided that Zedelph would have more influence on the public because he has a military background. I will be one of the people making decisions about the structure, policies and direction of our new nation from behind the scenes. I choose to be the silent, unseen hand that quietly makes things happen. This way I won't become a target of any potential enemies.

We had Zedelph appear on the national airwaves and announce that we now have a new government regime and the country is now named Melantis. He also announced that all the white citizens who did not take up arms against the Black population, and were against the racial injustices, were going to be allowed to live in special communities.

We have designated communities set up for the white population to protect their numbers so they will not go extinct. These communities don't operate like the Black ghettos and townships they set up for the former victims of white supremacy. We are not depriving them of any resources.

Like the Moors who occupied parts of Europe in the Middle Ages, we are providing them with a high quality of life, with the best amenities. We will guarantee that they will not be treated unjustly under our leadership. As long as they have the full understanding that they will never be allowed to practice white supremacy against the global Black population again, they will have a safe and secure existence.

Some of the white supremacist who fought against us eventually surrendered. Many members of the white militia groups went into hiding. We quickly tracked most of them down. Some of them were killed on the spot. Many of them were transferred to certain detention centers. The most vicious of these white supremacists were sent to the Camp of the Saints in Florida. We got them to give us useful info while they are detained. We killed many of them after we received the info we needed.

ONE MONTH LATER: AUGUST 21st, 2079

WE HAVE OFFICIALLY ESTABLISHED THE new country of Melania as an independent sovereign nation. Many Eastern nations have recognized us as a new nation, and we plan on establishing trade agreements with them in the near future.

We have strengthened our political and trade relations with the country of Eredo. We are starting to send some of our trade resources over there to them.

Within our own nation, we are continuing to restructure the government and organize every detail in our society. Our first order of business is to redistribute the land to all the Black masses who have been forced to live cramped up in the townships around the country. We are going to make sure that people have the land they need to grow food, build homes, and generally be as productive as possible.

Because of our successful revolution, (which has been named The Melanin Rebellion by the international press), there are similar racial uprisings in multiple European nations, and the Black people there are inspired and emboldened by us. All the African nations are inspired by us as well, and they have expelled all the white supremacists from their countries.

We stand with these brothers and sisters globally, and we will continue to help produce justice all over the planet.